SE[...]
Norman Lock'[...]

On Th[...]

"Brilli[...] *The Boy in His Winter* [...]ty, story, and the alchemical effects of [...] capacity to be changed by the con[...]ually evolving world when it strikes fire against the mind's flint,' and by profoundly moving novels like this." —*NPR*

"[Lock] is one of the most interesting writers out there. This time, he re-imagines Huck Finn's journeys, transporting the iconic character deep into America's past—and future." —*Reader's Digest*

"To call [*The Boy in His Winter*] a work of fiction is to tell only part of the story. This book is as much a treatise on memory and time and the nature of storytelling and our collective national conscience.... Much of it wildly funny and extremely intelligent." —*Star Tribune*

"Lock plays profound tricks, with language—his is crystalline and underline-worthy—and with time, the perfect metaphor for which is the mighty Mississippi itself." —*Publishers Weekly* (starred review)

On *American Meteor*

"Sheds brilliant light along the meteoric path of American westward expansion.... [A] pithy, compact beautifully conducted version of the American Dream, from its portrait of the young wounded soldier in the beginning to its powerful rendering of Crazy Horse's prophecy for life on earth at the end." —*NPR*

"[Walt Whitman] hovers over [*American Meteor*], just as Mark Twain's spirit pervaded *The Boy in His Winter*.... Like all Mr. Lock's books, this is an ambitious work, where ideas crowd together on the page like desperate men on a battlefield." —*Wall Street Journal*

"[*American Meteor*] feels like a campfire story, an old-fashioned yarn full of rich historical detail about hard-earned lessons and learning to do right." —*Publishers Weekly* (starred review)

"*American Meteor* is, at its core, a spiritual treatise that forces its readers to examine their own role in history's unceasing march forward [and] casts new and lyrical light on our nation's violent past." —*Shelf Awareness for Readers* (starred review)

On *The Port-Wine Stain*

"Lock's novel engages not merely with [Edgar Allan Poe and Thomas Dent Mütter] but with decadent fin de siècle art and modernist literature that raised philosophical and moral questions about the metaphysical relations among art, science and human consciousness. The reader is just as spellbound by Lock's story as [his novel's narrator] is by Poe's.... Echoes of Wilde's *The Picture of Dorian Gray* and Freud's theory of the uncanny abound in this mesmerizingly twisted, richly layered homage to a pioneer of American Gothic fiction." —*New York Times Book Review*

"As polished as its predecessors, *The Boy in His Winter* and *American Meteor*. . . . An enthralling and believable picture of the descent into madness, told in chillingly beautiful prose that Poe might envy." —*Library Journal* (starred review)

"As lyrical and alluring as Poe's own original work, *The Port-Wine Stain* captures the magic, mystery, and madness of the great American author while weaving an eerie and original tale in homage to him." —*Foreword Reviews*

"This chilling and layered story of obsession succeeds both as a moody period piece and as an effective and memorable homage to the works of Edgar Allan Poe."
—*Kirkus Reviews*

On *A Fugitive in Walden Woods*

"*A Fugitive in Walden Woods* manages that special magic of making Thoreau's time in Walden Woods seem fresh and surprising and necessary right now. . . . This is a patient and perceptive novel, a pleasure to read even as it grapples with issues that affect the United States to this day." —**Victor LaValle**, author of *The Ballad of Black Tom* and *The Changeling*

"Bold and enlightening. . . . An important novel that creates a vivid social context for the masterpieces of such writers as Thoreau, Emerson, and Hawthorne and also offers valuable insights about our current conscious and unconscious racism."
—**Sena Jeter Naslund**, author of *Ahab's Wife* and *The Fountain of St. James Court; or, Portrait of the Artist as an Old Woman*

"Bursts with intellectual energy, with moral urgency, and with human feeling. . . . Achieves the alchemy of good fiction through which philosophy takes on all the flaws and ennoblements of real, embodied life." —*Millions*

"Demonstrates Lock's uncanny ability to inhabit historical figures and meticulously capture the vernacular of the time like a transcendentalist ventriloquist. . . . Offer[s] profound insights that sharpen our understanding of American history."
—*Booklist* (starred review)

On *The Wreckage of Eden*

"Perceptive and contemplative. . . . Bring[s] the 1840–60s to life with shimmering prose." —*Library Journal* (starred review)

"Lock deftly tells a visceral story of belief and conflict, with abundant moments of tragedy and transcendence along the way." —*Kirkus Reviews*

"The lively passages of Emily's letters are so evocative of her poetry that it becomes easy to see why Robert finds her so captivating. The book also expands and deepens themes of moral hypocrisy around racism and slavery. . . . Lyrically written but unafraid of the ugliness of the time, Lock's thought-provoking series continues to impress." —*Publishers Weekly*

"[A] consistently excellent series. . . . Lock has an impressive ear for the musicality of language, and his characteristic lush prose brings vitality and poetic authenticity to the dialogue." —*Booklist*

FEAST DAY
of the
CANNIBALS

FEAST DAY
of the
CANNIBALS

Norman Lock

Bellevue Literary Press
New York

First published in the United States in 2019 by
Bellevue Literary Press, New York

For information, contact:
Bellevue Literary Press
90 Broad Street
Suite 2100
New York, NY 10004
www.blpress.org

Library of Congress Cataloging-in-Publication Data
Names: Lock, Norman, 1950– author.
Title: Feast day of the cannibals / Norman Lock.
Description: First edition. | New York : Bellevue Literary Press, 2019. | Series: The
    American novels
Identifiers: LCCN 2017049430 (print) | LCCN 2017053627 (ebook) | ISBN 9781942658474
    (ebook) | ISBN 9781942658467 (softcover)
Subjects: LCSH: United States—Social life and customs—19th century—Fiction. |
    United States—HIstory—19th century—Fiction. | GSAFD: Biographical fiction. |
    Historical fiction.
Classification: LCC PS3562.O218 (ebook) | LCC PS3562.O218 F43 2019 (print) |
    DDC 813/.54—dc23
LC record available at https://lccn.loc.gov/2017049430

Bellevue Literary Press would like to thank all its generous
donors—individuals and foundations—for their support.

 This publication is made possible by the New York
State Council on the Arts with the support of Governor
Andrew M. Cuomo and the New York State Legislature.

Book design and composition by Mulberry Tree Press, Inc.

Manufactured in the United States of America
First Edition

1 3 5 7 9 8 6 4 2

paperback ISBN: 978-1-942658-46-7

ebook ISBN: 978-1-942658-47-4

For George and Harry Hub

The Town is taken by its rats—

. . . already we have been the nothing we dread to be.

Cannibals? who is not a cannibal?

—Herman Melville

FEAST DAY
of the
CANNIBALS

From 1869 until its completion on May 24, 1883, Washington Roebling, chief engineer of the Brooklyn Bridge supervised its construction from a bedroom window overlooking the East River.

On April 22, 1882, Shelby Ross, a customhouse appraiser serving under Herman Melville, visited Roebling.

PART ONE

JONAH & THE WHALE

Washington Roebling's Second-Story Room at 110 Columbia Heights, Brooklyn, April 22, 1882

How goes the great bridge? Will you finish it on time?

Yes, let's hope in *my* lifetime, too, Roebling. When the span is finally done, I'll be as thrilled as the next man, although Melville may not share in the general delirium, which is sure to greet its completion after so many years. The New York and Brooklyn Bridge, like Cunard's transatlantic steamers, augurs the end of the wild breed that spawned his Captain Ahab, as well as the seagoing rabble who, after having jumped ship, grew seedy and bedeviled on a godless island in the Pacific. Mark my words: One day writers will be setting their tales in Bushwick and their romances in Park Slope. Why, just the other day, he was telling me—

Who? Herman Melville! You seem distracted this morning, Roebling. Are you sure the work is going well? I'd hate to think there could be something to delay the grand opening—an eventuality your arithmetic didn't foresee. Perhaps you and your father relied too much on the mathematical

15

sciences. I would have confirmed their predictions by having my palm read or my horoscope cast—my house is Mars, though I've never been to war. I'd have consulted the Fox sisters or the Witch of Endor, as well as Pythagoras and Euclid. What will you do, Roebling, if on the day when the bridge is finally open its granite towers fall into the East River? God, what an embarrassment!

You're right, my friend: It *is* no laughing matter. I'm glad you agreed to see me. It's been a long time since we were boys together.

As many as that? We'd barely begun to— What were we talking about? I've lost the thread.

Melville—thank you. The strands of my thought have a tendency to tangle. Yours, I imagine, are as orderly and your ideas as rigorous as a Roebling wire cable. The scraps of your unfinished breakfast, on which that fly is about to fatten, remind me of a night I spent recently with him. By the way, Herman was disappointed not to have been allowed to see you when we came out from the city to visit last week. Your wife is a formidable doorkeeper. Frankly, I was surprised that you wrote to me after all this time.

Our work at the customs office finished for the day, Melville and I stopped at an eating house on Broadway. The chops arrived fairly running with blood and, after having sent them back to the kitchen, the conversation turned into an unwholesome channel, steered by Melville, who is as salted as a herring in a barrel of brine from his years at sea. Evidently reminded of cannibalism by the bloody pork, he lectured me on the abomination, which, he said, could be extenuated by duress. He insisted that it is not only a practice among the headhunters of the Typee Valley, but was also a necessary last resort of the Donner Party, entombed by snow at Truckee Lake. This point of no return, where will and the appetite for life become predominant, has always fascinated him.

Did you ever eat at the Carberry? Noxious place—the plates are shiny with grease.

"I'm not always good company," said Melville, his gaze transfixed by gaslight playing on his knife.

I shrugged as if to say Who in his right mind is?

"I've nothing against you, Shelby. Lately, I've been preoccupied. Forgive me if I cannot share my thoughts." He looked up from his knife and said with a show of bonhomie, "You may ask me a question—anything within reason. No man can be entirely frank, not even with his wife. Perhaps her most of all. So what would you like to know? You may find out something useful that you can use for your advancement."

He sensed my indignation and apologized. "I beg your pardon. Life has given me reason to be cynical."

"Was it the War of the Rebellion that made you so?"

"All wars are boyish, and are fought by boys. The fratricide went on without me."

Later, I heard that his eyes, age, and a debilitating sciatica had kept Melville safely apart from the era's greatest misadventure, which he'd have joined otherwise, hoping to find in its strife and tumult a whetstone with which to sharpen his dulled appetite.

"Not that anyone cares. The world has forgotten me.

Nowadays, my comings and goings are known only to the fraternity of shopkeepers to whom I owe money. Poor Lizzie takes the brunt of their humiliating treatment." He rubbed the rim of his ear with a finger and said, "But perhaps you are curious about a morsel of gossip juicier than groceries."

Melville keeps most things to himself, although by this time I'd heard rumors about his past. I wondered if the memory of unspeakable feast days had struck a spark of madness in him. His eyes, as he regarded me across the table, had the unnatural brightness, the hectic quality of a lunatic's. As we waited for our chops to be brought from the kitchen, I nearly asked him if he had ever eaten human flesh. Instead, I coughed and took a drink of water.

Roebling, do you see those two women on the sidewalk standing next to the large policeman?

In their crinolettes and whalebone, they look like overladen ships. If I were to call down to them and ask if either could imagine a case in which she'd forget her Christian self and eat her companion on the hoof or—to be less repulsive—steal the other's diamond brooch to appease a gnawing hunger, how do you suppose she would answer me?

Just so! I suspect they have never known a hunger that could not be satisfied with a Thompson Chocolate. At my lowest and most dismal, I've felt a razor in my gut for want of what the butcher might put by for a mongrel dog. I ought to give those well-fed ladies one of Melville's books to chew on. It would be a very different sort of meal than any they have eaten heretofore, although I doubt either of them would read it after having seen the author's name on the spine, which they would not recognize. Ah, for a meal of Mrs. Radcliffe!

"Herman, I wonder what's keeping our supper," I said, trying to gather my wits.

As if in answer, the landlord returned with our plates—the offending meat transmuted by fire into something like shoe leather. Thus do our inferiors exact their revenge. Still at a loss for an answer to Melville's invitation, I made a show of mashing my potato with a fork.

"Well?" he said, his eyes boring into mine like gimlets. You would never have guessed that they troubled him. "Aren't you in the least curious about my past?"

I wanted to ask him how he could be vain enough to think I ought to be. He had a sense of his own worth—buried, as it was, at the bottom of his soul, where the muck is. For whatever reason, it had surfaced in that smoky chophouse, like a boat raised up from the ocean floor after it's been scuttled. I felt sorry for the man. Without his knowing, he'd revealed a secret about himself; I had stumbled onto his shame.

"I can't think of a single thing to ask you," I replied.

He let the matter drop, and for a while we gave ourselves to the conspicuous chewing of the overdone meat. The conversation became idle and desultory, confined to subjects that did not interest either of us. At last, it lost impetus, like flotsam caught in a slack tide, and silence fell over our small corner of the chophouse.

"Herman," I said, putting down my knife and fork in irritation. "Do you have anything to ask *me*?"

"Do you have anything worth my knowing?" he replied,

but not in the way you're thinking, Roebling. There was no mockery in his voice. He might even have spoken kindly, as one man would to another whose life could only have seemed pointless in his estimation. Perhaps he had come to believe that every man's life—every woman's, too—was, finally, empty.

I was determined to keep my secrets, harmless or otherwise, to myself. I don't know why I'm telling them to you. Weighed against that marvel of yours on the river, my life amounts to scarcely anything at all. A feather, or a reed uprooted from the muddy bottom by the tide and left to float among stone towers—that, Roebling, is what I am, or would be if, having foreseen it, the ancient Greeks had turned my life into a myth—a reed, or a feather, such as might have belonged to one of Icarus's wings, fashioned of wax and feathers by his father to escape the gravity of Crete.

Not mine! *Your* father was Daedalus, and you are his ambitious son. My father and I were no better than prospectors grubbing in the dirt in the hope of finding another Comstock Lode. I briefly ascended, like Icarus, only to fail and fall—unlike you. Which of us, I wonder, has paid the higher price for his vaulting ambition? I, who lost a fortune, or you, who very nearly lost your life and now must endure a life of pain?

If you were to unwind the history of the continent, like one of your steel cables, you'd find four strands: egalitarianism, self-reliance, contempt for nice manners and clean linen, and violence. While my linen may have been clean, my hands have not always been so. I was not one of Louisa May Alcott's "little men," unless it was Jack Ford, the rapscallion who robbed another schoolboy and allowed two others to take the blame. Jack was only following in his uncle's footsteps. I followed in those of my father, whose shoes were too fine-grained and costly to admit propinquity with a cow.

If you have the price of a loaf of bread, you needn't go hungry. If you have the price of a bottle of whiskey, you needn't be sober when the spur pricks. And in wartime, if you have three hundred dollars, you can buy another man to do your fighting—dying, too, if it comes to that—or your son's if you covet immortality by perpetuating your lineage or business. These lessons were taught me by my father, who, thanks to shrewd dealings and an occasional sharp practice, managed to organize the world around him in a way satisfactory to himself.

Father saw himself as a merchant prince, but he was only a carpetbagger rolling a small fortune made during the War of Secession into a large one after Lee's surrender at Appomattox. A New Englander, by nature sensitive and by inclination upright and humorless, Mother was not a suitable consort for a New York swank and sometime cutthroat sporting the gaudy fobs and garish waistcoats of an upstart and the ruthlessness of a marauder. Her heart gave out in February 1864, at the beginning of her husband's ascension. My brother, Charles junior, had died in the Draft Riots, a victim of his snobbish curiosity and of an Irishman beside himself with liquor chased by a hatred more bitter than hops. After Father's death in 1874, only I was left to carry on the Ross name and mercantile business, which had thrived on margins, fraud, if it could not be avoided, and the disregard of certain of the lesser commandments.

I proved an able steward of Charles's money, meaning I did not merely preserve the firm's capital, but enlarged it. My transgressions were readily overlooked by the stalwarts of capitalism: bankers, traders, financiers, and utilitarian philosophers, who were happy to leave ethical considerations to the theologians. Before the depression that followed the panic of '73 beggared me, my company had been the pride of investors and a plum of speculators.

Were I to publish the story of my life, literary critics would condemn me as an untrustworthy witness to events and a most unattractive character to boot. But as Emerson once said, "No picture of life can have any veracity that does not admit the odious facts." I'm not of a metaphysical bent and haven't read much by Emerson or those of his ilk. Their sensibilities are too refined for my taste. But Melville reads them, and I've spent enough time in his company to become acquainted with the Transcendentalists. I don't begrudge him his intellect any more than he does me the fortune I once possessed, nor does he vilify me for having once set aside as childish many of the scruples on which a righteous man preens himself.

Roebling, you seem restless. Do my revelations distress you? Or is it dyspepsia? You've been making a sour face. Are you certain the bridge is progressing as it should? Give me the glass, and I'll see for myself. The Dutch still make excellent lenses, though I can't see a thing through your dirty windows. You'd think that the New York Bridge Company could hire a man to keep them clean. How do they expect you to direct the work from this distant vantage if you cannot properly see? It's warm today. Shall I open a window?

There. The world is a little less occult with the sash thrown open. Let me see ... The men are working. God Almighty, I would rather jump off the pier in desperation than climb those towers! There're two little fellows standing on top of the Brooklyn-side tower, though I suppose that, in actuality, they're a pair of strapping camerados such as Walt Whitman loves. They say his poems are obscene. I wouldn't know. Melville often has his nose in them. I don't recall having read much modern verse, save for Whittier's *Snow-Bound* and Longfellow's *The Song of Hiawatha*.

Like most fathers of the upstart aristocracy, mine wanted a classical education for his sons. I saw no reason to object, so I enrolled in Manhattan College and was dosed with dead languages, ancient literature, and natural history, as well as enough law to circumvent it in the pursuit of my commercial interests. I came to know more about the Caesars and their high jinks than Boss Tweed and his villainies or about the comedies of Aristophanes than the farce being played daily in Tammany Hall. I could've told you more about the mastodon than the Mormons.

Despite such useless erudition, I learned what made a business hum. I read Chitty's *A Practical Treatise on Bills of Exchange, Checks on Bankers, Promissory Notes, Bankers' Cash Notes, and Bank Notes; Hunt's Merchants' Magazine;* Stevens's *Commercial History of the City of New York; Bradstreet's;* and the *Commercial Bulletin*. I pored over Burnham's *A Hundred Thousand Dollars in Gold: How to Make It* but found it as impracticable as Emerson's essay "Success." For pleasure, I read a number of Charles Dickens's novels, admittedly with more sympathy for Mr. Murdstone than David Copperfield and for Scrooge than his put-upon and cringing clerk.

Since my bankruptcy, the belief in economic imperialism is no longer salient in my character, and I now find myself sentimentally inclined toward the "surplus population," of which, in my present circumstances, I am one. I was in the same leaky boat as an out-of-print author named Melville and an out-of-luck former president named Grant. The three of us were bobbing together like old wine corks in a rain-swollen gutter. To keep one's head above water is the constant preoccupation of anybody who has sunk into the dark and treacherous depths where piranhas lurk.

Melville and I visited Grant when he was living on the Upper East Side, his time run out and fire nearly quenched. I admired him, and his insolvency was a comfort to me in mine. If the life of a former commanding general of the Union army and chief executive of the United States could be written in red ink, a merchant could pardon himself for his own embarrassment. Melville presented him with a copy of his book *Battle-Pieces and Aspects of the War*. On the frontispiece, he'd written:

> To General U.S. Grant,
> "A good man's fortune may grow out at heels;
> Give you good morrow!"
> —Kent to King Lear
>
> HERMAN MELVILLE
> March 21, 1882

I don't know why Melville asked me to go with him, unless he wanted to show off his connections. I have his Civil War poems, although I've yet to read them. The inscription falls far short of the genuinely tragic sentiment he penned for Grant. Mine, in fact, is downright farcical. I suppose I deserved no better than he gave.

> To Shelby Ross, Former Gent,
>
> Who Shares My Chain
> In Chester Arthur's Leaky Galley.
>
> HERMAN MELVILLE
> New York City, March 15, 1882

One thing I know, Roebling: Your bridge is magnificent and deserving of universal praise, though the naysayers and skeptics decry it. One day it will be your cenotaph. It ought to be called "Roebling Bridge," but perhaps you lack the vainglory of the scribbler who must affix his name to every scrap of paper dirtied by his hand. I wonder if, in ages hence, your bridge will be this country's pyramid and sphinx. Strung like a harp, it would be the perfect instrument for one of Whitman's rhapsodies, but he prefers the Brooklyn ferry, where he can loaf at the rail and confab with this man and that woman, breathing them in, their scent, their atmosphere, while winding his arms about them. I can see it steaming toward the Fulton slip, although not as he would, if he were here with us, crowding the room with his democratic enthusiasm, his sheer animalism. Whitman looks with other eyes than those of a customhouse appraiser or an engineer.

Take the glass. Do you see the ferryboat nearing the Manhattan tower? What an infernal thing it is, throwing acres of crepe into the air behind it as it goes! The steam age is not a golden one, I fear. It's as romantic as a boiler and as unpleasant to the ear as a jaw harp or a "circus screamer."

Are you comfortable? I can't imagine being anchored to a chair and obliged to watch your greatest work raised up by others through a telescope. I admire your courage. Standing beside you, I feel like one of Louisa May's "little men" after all. You are Jonah, stricken with misfortune and thrust into the belly of a great fish. So, too, is Melville, who labors in a darkness of his own—barred from life by the enormous teeth of a cruel engine that gins him fine. Unless he gnaws on himself, like a dry biscuit. Roebling, we are all Jonases—shut up inside our own thoughts, as if in rooms needing to be aired. I'm the frightened one who prays to be let out of his caisson into the air and light of day. One minute I curse God as Ahab did Moby Dick; the next I beseech Him.

What's that you say?

No, I'm not Shadrach, Meshach, *or* Abednego. My fiery furnace is cold, and I suspect Melville's is, too. I almost envy you. Your work is far more important than enforcing the excise tax. You look out through the window and see a bridge being knit out of cables, as surely as a woman plying her needles watches a garment taking shape before her eyes, while I make rows of numbers in a ledger. Melville has his stanzas and paragraphs, which add up to something, I suppose. For

me, life—what's left of it to call my own—consists of subtraction. Self-pity is delicious, is it not? Even you must succumb to it now and then. I know Melville does, though he
tries to keep it to himself like a bittersweet confection one
would rather not share. Adversity will make a man as hard as
an oyster shell or as tender as the animal inside it.

You are fortunate in your wife, Roebling. She has stood
by you all these years after you lost your health. From what
Melville has told me, Emily does more than carry your
instructions to the men at work. She must be an extraordinary woman to have become far more valuable to you
than a nurse or an amanuensis. She kept your bridge alive,
or else there'd be nothing to see through the window but
the unbroken surface of the East River, where the massive
columns rise.

No, I never married.

No, there was no one. I was fascinated by business and
my own sense of growing worth and power. For a time, they
occupied me constantly, to borrow from Ebenezer Scrooge.
I'd have made a bad husband and a worse father.

I'm almost forty—not much younger than you are, however aged our appearances. We burned the candle at both
ends—mine, I'm embarrassed to say, guttered down on the
altar of self-regard, first in the carelessness of youth and then
in whatever mischief a man can make in his "money-chang-
ing hole," to quote old Jacob Marley. After the war, Father
converted one of his factories, in which iron-wire cradles for
the limbs of wounded soldiers in Union hospitals had been
made, to the manufacture of steel-caged crinolines to support

a lady's skirts. Our wallets bulged, as they had on the profits netted by four years of ghastly wounds and amputations.

Do I feel remorse?

That's a question better left to a priest or a judge to ask. I don't believe in a salvation granted in the nick of time. It was one thing for Jesus to tell the repentant sinner on his cross, "To day shalt thou be with me in paradise," and a very different matter for a priest, with holy oil and viaticum, to wipe a life's dirty slate clean. Likewise to do a stretch in prison is hardly a fair exchange for having committed some villainy.

To say what I would do, given a second chance, is speculation grounded in regret and terror of what is likely to befall me. But despite my weariness, I'm a young man still, or, if not young, then only a little way past my day's high noon. Who knows, Roebling? I may yet make something of myself! In a gloomy hold below the waterline, I can examine my life and—to be honest, it will probably come to naught; the New York Custom House is not a place where a man can accomplish much.

I'm not cut out for a martyr's life, or a monk's, either; to put on sackcloth would be mere ostentation. I hope to be as Whitman is or Lincoln was: a man of the world. By that, I mean a man very much *in* the world, unconcerned by the raised eyebrow, the haughty, upturned nose, and the cold shoulder of disdain. My indifference to respectability is a far cry from a youthful ambition to hobnob with an Astor or a Vanderbilt.

It's troubling to have so much wealth pass through my hands, and not a penny of it sticks. I'm paid a meager salary—three dollars for a day's drudgery. After fifteen years in the service, Melville takes home only a dollar a day more. With cunning, I could line my pockets as Chester Arthur did his before becoming our twenty-first president. So far I've resisted the temptation to embezzle, as the saint did the fleshpots of Egypt, only not so readily. Meanwhile, Melville and I rub along together in mutual discontent. The customhouse, Roebling, is just another caisson in which men are shut up and left to scrabble for light, air, and a larger sense of purpose.

You could have renounced yours and left the bridge for someone else to build. But here you've toiled all these years, enclosed within four walls. Well, every man and woman inhabits a caisson, if it comes to that. We drag out our lives in the belief that we are not alone. I talk to God, though He has little to say to me. Sometimes I feel oppressed, as if I had the weight of the river on my chest. Life must weigh more heavily on someone like you, who was an aeronaut during the war. To have been lighter than air, suspended in a basket, high above the hills and trees! It surely was an ecstasy to see the world in miniature unrolling before you—Lee's Army of Northern Virginia reduced to specks, to ants marching in formation toward the Union anthills. The workmen swarming over the bridge's columns and steel webs must see humanity from the same inhuman perspective. The city shall be raised up into the sky by men, and humankind will be belittled by comparison. That is progress, my friend; that is the future being made before our very eyes.

To put one's trust in a telescope takes a leap of faith

because we can never be sure that the magnified world seen through its lens is not an illusion. Your granite towers seem real enough for birds to sit upon. Birds, which are skeptical of cats and men, have faith that an avian Providence will supply worms and crumbs when they are hungry and a stone ledge when they're in need of rest. But what if the meager repast and the aerial perch exist nowhere except in the expectations of a bird? A frivolous question for a builder, who is, and must be, a materialist. Ah, well, Roebling. Like most of humanity, I myself have built nothing lasting.

Naturally, you are curious about Melville. Having nowhere to go this afternoon, I'll tell you what I know of him—and what I know of myself, which is not so much as I like to think and more than I would care to acknowledge. The truth is too often what we hide from ourselves. Let's leave it to our biographers to weed and prune our lives and the storytellers to shape them.

I'm in the mood to talk. The last week has been—well, disturbing. And the disease that sapped you of energy has made you an excellent audience. You don't waste words or, as some others do, bristle with opinions of your own. I'll begin my story on the pier where I met Melville for the first time, by the North River—or the Hudson, as it's also called.

I know, I know, but it'll be easier if I tell it as the words occur to me. Just pretend you're in a Chautauqua tent, listening to a man ramble on about his life to strangers.

U.S. Customs Office at 207 West Street, Near the North River, January 3, 1882

Early in the new year, I took up my duties in a small rented office on West Street, near the North River. Had I been assigned to the U.S. Custom House itself, on Wall Street, with its twelve Ionic columns of Quincy granite and marble floors, I would not have felt so reduced by circumstances—which were beyond my control, mind you! My pride was raw after the loss of my money, business, a fine apartment, and polite society, which now shunned me. On that dismal winter morning, I had dressed carefully in order to make a good impression on my superiors. My frock coat, fancy waistcoat, and striped trousers—suitable for a Wall Street financier, though not a customhouse drudge—were elegantly cut; my snowy linen bore the diamond studs I'd not yet pawned. As I walked along Gansevoort Pier, the roughnecks busying themselves among the ships, bales, barrels, hogsheads, and swaybacked dray horses hitched to overloaded wagons could have mistaken me for a shipowner, or a man from Lloyd's.

I had spent my remaining "capital," accrued during prosperous times, to obtain the position of customhouse appraiser, insignificant as it was. In moneyed days, I had had an acquaintance—I'll call him Clifford. We were not close, but more than once, each of us had witnessed the other compromising his integrity. He was related in the round-about way of large families to Henry Clay Frick, who had recently multiplied his fortune by joining his coke resources to Andrew Carnegie's steel mills. Having read of his business coup in the papers, I asked Clifford to approach his relation on my behalf. He demurred until I reminded him of a girl in Frank Woolworth's Great Five Cent Store in Utica. Not long after this spur, I was hired as an appraiser and assigned to the busy North River pier, where Melville served as district inspector.

When I swaggered into the customs office for the first time, Melville was poring over a grimy document. He barely acknowledged my presence in the cramped space we two would be sharing. The atmosphere was rank with his cigar smoke. I coughed gravely and deliberately to let him know I found the stink of his stogie offensive. I may even have wrinkled my patrician nose in disgust, like a monkey given something disagreeable to eat.

He looked up at me and said, "Hang your coat and hat in the closet—and mind your wet shoes. Next time, use the boot scraper."

Having put my things in a closet containing waterproofed boots, oilskin capes, and tarpaulin hats intended for the prosecution of our official duties in rain and snow, I sat behind a desk offering a cheerless view of dirty gray sky seen through unwashed panes of glass. Melville took up his pen and returned to the document that had been occupying him. I took up a book from the desk and, to quiet my nerves, began to read the rules and regulations of my new trade. For some reason, the sound of Melville's pen scratching on a gray sheet a lengthy paragraph of dreary, arid prose (an inventory of tonnage) disheartened me.

If I'd read his books, I might have wondered that a hand

that had written of Ishmael, Ahab, and Moby Dick did not rebel against the poor use to which it had been put. That bleak morning, however, I didn't know the history of his successes or his failures, nor how very near we were in circumstances. I saw only a handsome, if weary, man wearing a blue serge jacket, with the tin badge of a customs inspector pinned to the lapel. I gave him what I judged to be a winning smile as I waited to receive my instructions. In that he did not choose to interrupt his writing until the final period had been applied with an emphatic rap, I studied him the while with an insolent disregard for good manners.

He has intelligent blue eyes, amused and even a little contemptuous, set in an oval face. His complexion is fair; the features are regular and fine; his hair and beard, once brown, have turned gray. A noble brow crowns a head such as Rodin could, without reservation, sculpt and set beside his *Saint John*. He has something of Robert E. Lee about him—not the face, but the military bearing, despite the rheumatism that pains him. You'd think he'd been to the academy at West Point, although he must sometimes depend upon a cane.

Tired of being kept waiting, I cleared my throat.

Melville went on a little farther down the page and then put down his pen.

"The streets round about are as thick with cutthroats as fleas on a dog. They'll have you, liver and lights, to get those fancy studs." He had sized me up as if I were an item of contraband.

Embarrassed, I tried to make a joke of it, and failed, not having an aptitude for humor.

He leaned back in his chair. "I was told to expect Mr. Ross, the new appraiser for Gansevoort Pier—a position secured, no doubt, by a friend's influence, a bribe, a dodge, or other shady dealings. Would you be the gent?"

"I am," I said, half amused and half abashed.

"Good," he said with a nod, whose tenor I could not guess. "Please excuse an excess of caution, but you can appreciate my wariness when, expecting a lowly customs 'coney catcher,' I see standing before me a man dressed for a Freemasons' ball or a gathering of Tammany henchmen."

He sensed my annoyance and relaxed his small mouth into a grin.

"I had Henry Smythe to grease the ways for me. He ended by sliding ignominiously down the slippery slope of corruption, from the collector of customs to an impeached embezzler. My name is Melville, district inspector of knavery and chicanery, both abundant in the great city of Babylon on the Hudson. Welcome to the asylum of non-entities." He opened a drawer and took out a tin badge like his, except for the word *appraiser* stamped into the metal. "Your aegis," he said. "In the closet, you'll find the blue jacket of our fraternal order."

I exchanged my frock coat for the jacket and felt, all at once, disgraced as the reality of my new situation struck me. I pinned on the customs badge and understood that I had cast off, like a snake its skin, an old self no longer fitting or useful. Tomorrow, I told myself, I'll pawn the studs.

"You'd better put on a pair of sea boots while you're at it," he called from his desk. "The leftover snow will spoil your fine gaiters."

I looked at my shoes and saw that they had already been ruined by my preposterous stroll along Gansevoort Pier.

"You'll be outdoors a good part of the day."

"My predecessor had big feet," I said, returning to my chair.

"He did, though in every other way he was a little man. He was sacked for taking bribes, which are ubiquitous in our service. You'll be offered the Devil's own temptations, and it takes a Jesus Christ sometimes to resist them."

I felt my lips compress in mockery.

"Believe me, Mr. Ross, I am not He. I'm simply afraid, and fear is as good a stick to beat the Devil as a cross. Honesty does not belong exclusively to the virtuous."

"You might call me by my Christian name," I said, "if we're to be cribbed together."

"Which might be what?"

"Shelby."

"An unusual name for a man, although I knew a Shelby in Atlanta before the war."

I shrugged my shoulders as if to say, I've heard it all before.

"Call me Herman." He glanced at me, as if expecting me to smirk, but at the time, I was deaf to the echo of his famous sentence concerning Ishmael.

Do you see, Roebling, how soured life in the modern age has become that irony should be our frequent response to it? But as I said, the name Herman Melville meant nothing to me then, nor had I heard of his novels. *Moby-Dick*, remember, had been published in 1851, and by 1880, it had fairly sunk from view.

"What is it that an appraiser does?"

Melville found the question comical. "Why, appraise!"

"It's an honest question!" I replied irritably.

"As befits an honest man," he said with a smile, which threatened to become a sneer. "The appraiser verifies that a merchant has not undervalued his goods in order to reduce the duty due upon delivery—in our case, at the Port of New York."

He glanced through the dirty window at the sky, which was lowering.

"In that dishonesty is acknowledged to be a universal trait of our kind, the Customs Service has incorporated suspicion and mistrust into its machinery. Nonetheless, goods are still pilfered, and fraud is practiced. Thus do we find ourselves working inside a model of a universe, obedient to an intangible malignity, where honest dealings are the exception that proves the rule. You may have your own ideas concerning the moral nature of humankind and the harsh view the U.S. Customs Service and I take of it. But I'm obliged, by long experience, to take a dim one."

Melville is a man of integrity, who, because of it, has eluded the new brooms of five administrations—a rarity in the service, where officers and clerks seem to be chosen for an aptitude in thievery. He could have dragged himself and his family out of everlasting debt and found time, which our occupational exhaustion denies him, to write more books. And yet he has never embezzled, winked at smuggling schemes, or taken bribes from crooked merchants and shipping firms. Not that he's a saint. No, I would not care to spend any length of time with one, since few of us wish to be reminded of our sins.

Melville looked into my eyes with the intensity of a mesmerist. I lowered them and regarded my fingernails, which were pink and immaculate. Soon enough, they would be black and broken.

"The New York City docks and its customhouse produce half the revenue of all other United States ports combined. Money is a magnet, whose attractions few can resist. Humankind is a self-serving species, Mr. Ross, and its appetites are gargantuan."

"Shelby," I said with seeming irrelevance.

"Pardon?"

"Won't you please call me by my Christian name?"

"You are a Christian, then?" Before I could reply, he said, "No matter."

I considered Melville's attitude toward his fellows misanthropic. As cynical as the years had made me, I had yet to wish myself a member of another species, which, according to Charles Darwin's book, was likely to be as brutish as our own. I accept the Fall and the tatty unraveling of God's gift. Who faults a tree for the crookedness of some of its branches? Who considers the tiger's appetite for flesh immoral? Who fulminates against the fish, which never looks to heaven until it's yanked up on a string? Men and women are imperfect creatures and, therefore, natural. Didn't

Emerson and Thoreau accept payment from the lyceums for extolling nature's virtues? What were they but a pair of moral philosophers for hire? And so I admit that when five thousand crates of green oranges from the Azores arrived on the *Fredonia* last week, I took a crate and sold it. It's common for a customs officer to pilfer a bottle of Barbados rum to stave off the winter chill. I've seen Melville take a French silk ribbon for his wife and a bottle of vintage Madeira for his lunch. To filch a ribbon or even a crate of oranges is nothing compared to stealing a hundred imperial yards of Irish linen—gold at a time when our domestic fabrics are little better than tow cloths.

Washington Roebling. You, too, must be burdened by your given name. Does it keep you honest? Did you never take something that didn't belong to you? You know the rhyme "the kingdom was lost. And all for the want of a horse-shoe nail." Surely you wouldn't hesitate to steal a nail—or a whole horse—to finish a bridge?

"I take it you have the necessary qualifications for the post of customs appraiser?" asked Melville with a straight face.

"At one time, I owned a business of my own," I replied—haughtily, I admit.

"What happened to it?"

"It went into receivership."

We paused briefly to listen to the rain beating on the roof.

"Then you were either an honest man or a fool," he said.

"Let's say I was an honest fool and leave it at that." In truth, I was sometimes honest and sometimes foolish.

My gaze fell on a harpoon standing in a corner of the office, next to a cabinet containing rolled-up nautical charts.

"Do whales inhabit the North River?"

"I keep it for the rats," replied Melville, having taken no notice of my flippancy. "If ever you are called upon to descend into the hold of a ship from Canton, I recommend that you go armed; Chinese rats grow big as possums."

The door swung open, and a boarding inspector entered the room, scattering rain from his slicker.

"Mind the wet!" admonished Melville, covering a document with his sleeve. "You're leaking like an uncaulked skiff!"

The man grunted words—I doubt of apology. He slid a ship's manifest across Melville's desk and said, "The *Saxony*'s in port, loaded with barley and Hallertau hops for the Lispenard Brewery."

"Very well," said Melville.

The man left, closing the door behind him emphatically to let us know that he, too, was one of the camerados.

We put on our oilskins and went outside into the rain. The *Saxony* was berthed at the end of the pier, and I was already feeling miserable as we trudged along it, to an accompaniment of sounds peculiar to ports in foul weather. Winds played in the shrouds—ropes to landsmen—bells tolled, blocks clattered like wooden glockenspiels, gulls screeched, steam winches groaned, boatswains' whistles skirled, and sheets rang against masts: an orchestra conducted by men shouting into speaking trumpets. I didn't know it then, but Melville had heard the same raucous music in his youth, not as a minor official of the Customs Service, but as a sailor does a rousing overture to far-flung voyages. The pages of his books are loud with it, so steeped was he in the music of the piers—a clever trope, you must admit.

A WEIGHER WAS LEANING against a bollard when we arrived at the *Saxony,* which was riding low against the pier, in the murky water of the North River. Nests of reeds and trash bobbed alongside her hull.

"Mr. Gibbs, this is Mr. Ross, our new appraiser," said Melville. "Mr. Gibbs is an old hand and will show you what to do."

Gibbs scratched his hairy ear and nodded, as if Melville had just spoken of someone else.

The three of us boarded and climbed down into the hold, where a pungent odor of hops, coffee, mildewed grain, and bilge conspired to make my gorge rise.

Before the panic and ensuing depression, I hadn't an inkling of the destitution awaiting me. None could have foreseen it, not even if he'd read the palm of the "invisible hand," which Adam Smith called the unpredictable force that spites a planned economy, or glimpsed the future in a glass of beer. The future ruined Thomas Durant, whose Irishmen had laid the Union Pacific tracks from Council Bluffs west to Promontory Summit, where they'd met the Central Pacific's "coolies" and hammered home the golden spike. It ruined Jay Cooke, the financier, who'd also dreamed of building a railroad—his connecting Duluth with the Great Lakes. It ruined eighteen thousand businesses, including mine, and the only outfit to profit by it was the Ku Klux Klan. Misery converts desperate men to desperate causes.

In the funereal light of the hold, the weigher Gibbs sat down against a bulkhead and chewed a twist of tobacco while Melville walked among sacks stuffed with barley and hops, idly tapping them with a pencil. Now and then, he'd slit open the burlap with his pocketknife, plunge his hands into the sweet-smelling grain or brewers' spicy flowers, and sniff with the air of a connoisseur nosing a glass of single malt or a lady the sachet in a bureau drawer of dainties.

Gibbs is one of those men who appear to be loafing even when attending to their duties—an egalitarian pose encountered everywhere in our democracy, whose caroler is Walt Whitman.

Having finished his inspection, Melville climbed out of the hold and disappeared into a gray sky hung with rain. Each slow step upon the ladder appeared to have pained him. Gibbs spat tobacco juice after him in good riddance. Since he was in no hurry to instruct me in the priestly duties of our office, I sat down and contemplated my wet boots, which, thanks to Mr. Goodyear's genius, had kept my socks dry.

Do I have the determination to lift myself up by my boot-straps and begin life anew? I asked myself. From where I sat on a piece of burlap at the bottom of a suffocating hole in the river, renewal seemed impossible.

The panic, which had sunk the economy seven years earlier, did not ruin me overnight. My ship took time to go down— enough for me to step into a lifeboat instead of throwing myself into the sea. I sold stock my father had purchased imprudently and bought shares in more stable concerns. I had my surviving factory, which had been producing wire implements, converted for the manufacture of Glidden's barbed wire. I hoped to supply the farmers during their range war with the cattlemen. Unfortunately, the cattle business went to hell. By the time the country had recovered from the Gold Exchange and Jay Gould's "corner," I'd scuttled my ship and changed from canny businessman to bankrupt—from well-to-do to ne'er-do-well. As I told you, I kept my once-fashionable clothes and watched them grow shabby.

Do you feel a draft, Roebling? Let me close the window. Looks like rain in the here and now. Now back to my first dreary day on Gansevoort Pier. Having delayed as long as we dared, Gibbs weighed and I appraised the musty sacks chosen by the Captain Ahab of the customhouse.

My colleague was a squat man with surprisingly broad shoulders and large, hairy hands. I suppose he could be described as "simian." He had a repertory of unpleasant habits in addition to chewing tobacco, which had left a brown stain on his unkempt beard. I'd turn away in disgust when he cleared his nose of smut without benefit of handkerchief. I shrank from him each time he put a hand inside his trousers and scratched with the deliberateness of a flea-bitten dog. I was afraid vermin would jump from his clothes into mine, and that first night, I fumigated them in the airing closet at Mrs. McFadden's boardinghouse, where I lodged uncomfortably for four dollars a week, plus board. I took to smoking cheap, malodorous cigars, hoping to asphyxiate any pests acquired from the unsavory Mr. Gibbs.

Here comes the rain! You can't see a blessed thing outside. The whole world might be flooding. A second Deluge, eh, Roebling? To wash the world clean of our sins. I'd wager a year's pay that your bridge would have survived the Flood, along with Noah's ark. "And the Lord said, I will destroy man whom I have created from the face of the earth; both man, and beast, and the creeping thing, and the fowls of the air; for it repenteth me that I have made them." I don't blame the Lord for wanting to get rid of a botched job.

Yes, a "creeping thing" is Mr. Gibbs. Bear with me, Roebling. My stories resemble a tangle of anchor cable in a ship's chain locker, but the links are there to follow, one after the other notwithstanding.

Our work in the hold finished, Gibbs turned on me with a snarl. "By your finery, I'd say you were either a 'Mary' or a poet." In his mouth, the word *poet* took on the unsavoriness of a hermaphrodite. "Not that I've anything against lavender waistcoats, but it sickens me to see the way you strut like a damned politician or a nigger at a cotillion."

"I beg your pardon?" I could feel my cheeks flush.

"'I beg your pardon!'" he said mockingly. "You might think you were First Lord of His Majesty's Customs and Excise come to complain about the tea dumped into Boston Harbor by the Sons of Liberty." He spat, and I jog-stepped to avoid the spittle. "Or David come to bushwhack Jonathan." And then he spat at me again.

Enraged, I flailed at him absurdly, although I managed to bloody his drunkard's nose. Stunned, he blew red snot from his nostrils, and then, bellowing in pain, or fury, or both, he swung his longshoreman's hook at me. Had it met its mark, it would've pierced my skull as though it were a melon. In an instant—part impetuosity, part insanity—I reached for the knife Melville had left behind him—staff of office for those who risk life and limb in the pursuit of taxation—and lunged at Gibbs's chest. Out of my wits and my element, I caught him on his sleeve. Once again he roared. Although I dropped the knife in horror, I was thrilled to have nearly killed a man. I trembled in a delirium of ire and ecstasy. So this is what men feel who finally have done with the illusion and hypocrisy of civilization! I thought.

"I'll make you sorry you ever stuck your head out of your mother's fucking hole!" he hissed with a savagery I had not heretofore encountered in my fellow man.

I laughed nervously and started up the ladder, the back of my neck tingling in dread that at any moment I might be felled by a belaying pin. I did not turn to look at him, afraid of the power of his malignant gaze. With fear comes irrationality, and with it the blind credulity of the religiously minded. Though an alien one, juju is just another faith. If Gibbs catches my eye, I told myself as I climbed the ladder leading upward from the miniature hell, I'll be obliged to hang myself from the nearest beam.

Gibbs shouted another obscenity, and I knew that I had made an enemy of him.

Roebling's Second-Story Room on Brooklyn Heights, April 22, 1882

The newspapers are calling your bridge "one of the wonders of the world," equal to anything the ancients raised for all their thousands and tens of thousands of slaves. Here's a question to vex you: If the Union had lost the war and there'd been no emancipation, would you have used negro slaves instead of the city's Irish?

I haven't the slightest doubt that you're a principled man, Roebling; but can you honestly say that if the East River Bridge depended on the free labor of slaves for its completion, you'd give it up for a principle? There is always an unanswerable question, or one whose answer will turn the world upside down. It's the job of fools and philosophers to ask it.

Me? More fool than philosopher, although a plausible one. I've always had the silver tongue of a pulpit crooner or a confidence man.

The rain shows no sign of letting up. It must raise hell with your timetable. It makes working on the docks a sodden misery. But water is the primary and unconquerable element, as those who end up drowning find out. It douses fire, turns earth to mud and air to mist. "And God said, Let there be a firmament in the midst of the waters, and let it divide the waters from the waters." What fish, I wonder, can swim in the waters *above* the firmament? Moby Dick. Not that I believe the Bible stories, mind you. But I'd sooner wear studs of diamond or pearl than bone and read Genesis instead of Darwin or Charles Lyell. Our contemporaries' accounts of creation might well be the truth, but damn it if they're not as dry as the Host in the mouth of a communicant kneeling at the altar rail!

My father bought a choice pew in the old Cedar Street Presbyterian Church as he would have a seat on the stock exchange. The doctrines of predestination and election confirmed his self-interest. He could do nothing, he said, on behalf of the unfortunates, because God had forecast his every move, as if life were a horoscope and we were obedient to planetary aspects and conjunctions. I can see him even now, taking his ease in an upholstered chair—his coat off and waistcoat unbuttoned, revealing a paunch and a gold watch chain, and puffing at a fat cigar, the image of complacency. Father was not entirely a liar or a thief except as a man of business will sometimes be for the good of his shareholders and confederates. They propped one another up, and not a man among them could have foreseen the day when the props would be kicked out from under them. Father was no more evil than Ahab, although they sometimes did evil things in their separate wars against fatality. Madness and Calvinism are difficult burdens to bear, and both an offense to reasonable men.

Am I? Well, hairs are meant to be split. That's another thing I've learned. Didn't Polk fuddle the line between the purchase of Mexican territory and its theft? Disgruntled Americans living in another sovereign nation have only to complain that their lives and property are at risk to cause a battalion of marines to sally forth in defense of their interests.

One man's robbery is another's brilliant coup, just as surely as "spotted dick" is another name for suet pudding.

What will you do, Roebling, when the bridge is done? It's been your abiding concern since your father, dying of tetanus, left you to finish it. You were both casualties to ambition—or perhaps retribution. The Almighty might not have cared to have His works rivaled by one of His creatures. What can you turn your hand to next that won't be the death of you? You look played out, like a mine after its ore has been picked clean. Well, we have that much in common—you, Melville, Grant, and I. Pity we don't play whist; we'd make a dour foursome.

When I was a boy of seven or eight, I watched my father being sick. It was just an ordinary cold on the stomach or griping of the guts, such as you and I have suffered a hundred times in our lives. I remember being surprised that he should have been changed in an instant from a crusty, capable man, who each morning dressed and took a horsecar to his office in Greenwich Street and who sat on the Board of Brokers and the Alms House Hospital, into a puking, groaning infant. He lay helplessly on the floor of his bedchamber, heaving his guts into a chamber pot while I gazed in fascination at his abasement. Afterward, when he was able to stand and wipe the vomit from his lips and had changed into clean clothes, he said to me, "We are made sick to remind us of what we were and are and will be." A boy, I did not understand. I knew only that I had seen my father humiliated, as Ham had seen his father, Noah, naked and asleep after having drunk too much wine. What I could not have put into words—not then and hardly now—was the sense of giddiness I felt. The world had been stood on its head. I'd seen my father lying on the floor, careless of his dignity.

Roebling, you must have seen the like when your father died in agony, after his foot had been crushed by a Fulton Street ferry and the gangrene had done its dreadful work. Now here you sit, as you have done for a dozen years and more, a shut-in on your quarterdeck, where you are hobbled like Captain Ahab by his ivory leg—an "*Isolato*," as Melville, in his book, called a man who occupies his own separate continent.

When a life ends prematurely or horrifically, we call it a "tragedy," whether the victim is Oedipus the king or a woman who falls down a flight of stairs and breaks her neck. Just so, we have to make do with the word *slaughter* to describe the killing of ten thousand men in battle or a chicken in the dooryard. Is our language so poor that we cannot find a word to distinguish the magnitude of death or sin? What an old-fashioned word is *sin*! It doesn't seem to belong to the modern world of transatlantic steamers and telegraph cables, elevated trains and the Roebling bridge. Whenever I say *sin* to myself, I think of Nathaniel Hawthorne's *The Scarlet Letter* and "Young Goodman Brown." Sin was real to him. At one time, Melville was very much attached to Hawthorne. The attachment may have been the most profound of his life. The friendship was short-lived, although Melville still thinks of the older man, dead these twenty years or so. Inside his house, he gives Hawthorne's books pride of place in a cabinet, along with his hand-tinted ambrotype. An accidental friendship is either an alloy that strengthens character or else a corrosive that destroys it.

In time, of course, all things erode, rot, molder, or rust, according to the material. Your bridge has already started on the process of disintegration. Many hands will be kept busy in the future, chipping and painting—labor for a modern Sisyphus and a monument to futility. You wonder why the stars have not worn out their orbits' grooves when—according to the town of Rawlins, Wyoming, the gates of Paradise would rust were it not for the Rawlins Red oxide paint on them. And still the East River flows everlastingly onward into the bay, and the bay carries its atoms to the ocean.

What do you think, Roebling? Will the river one day dry up and with it the bay? Will the oceans shrink and unearth continents of mud? Or will the polar regions melt, and the rising seas sweep us back to creation's fifth day, when God created great whales?

The Melvilles' House at 104 East Twenty-sixth Street, April 15, 1882

Last week, Melville, who had been reserved, even distant, invited me home to dinner. At six o'clock, having finished the day's work, we walked east on Thirteenth Street to Fifth Avenue, then north to Madison Square Park, where federal troops had once bivouacked during the Draft Riots of 1863.

"My elder brother, Charles, was murdered in the riots," I said. "The mob dragged him from a horsecar and beat him to death with paving stones."

"The Town was taken by its rats!" snarled Melville.

"A mick wrote an insulting squib on the wall next to

Charles's body: 'For sale. Three hundred dollars' worth of prime meat.'"

We sat on an iron bench in the park. Melville seemed reluctant to go home. He's a taciturn man, embittered by ill fortune and lost fame. Yet you could almost say he enjoys his failure as some people do the burning of a gum rubbed with salt. Night was drawing near, and the darkness had begun to sprawl. Edison's incandescent lamps had yet to light the city, which, until that time, would shelter what flourishes in the shadows.

Edison, Westinghouse, Charles Brush, and you, Roebling, and your father before you—where does it come from, the inspiration, genius, gift—call it what you will—that gives into your hands the lever by which to move the world? Why you and not some others? And why should Melville fail and Samuel Clemens thrive? Why should Grant become a pauper when the war's great joke, George McClellan, became chief engineer of the New York City Docks and then the governor of New Jersey? And while I'm asking God to justify his nepotism, why am I a three-dollar-a-day clerk swallowed up by the cold or stifling holds of ships? I'm in the belly of a whale, and it intends to keep me there. My pain is nothing next to yours, Roebling. But by God, there is nothing so salutary as the tears we shed for ourselves! They are the brine in which our aborted plans and failures are pickled.

In the park, a night bird spoke to me in Bird of the bitterness of winter snows. Thus is a happy moment buried under past regrets.

"Do you know what a 'gam' is?" asked Melville.

"No."

"It's a kind of church social for whaling men when two ships chance upon each other. It relieves the boredom of a long sea voyage. Boredom is the worst of it. A sailor will sooner tolerate lice and fleas, hardtack and rancid pork, cockroaches in the molasses, the slimy black walls, stench, and heat of the fo'c'sle. When men are shut up together for three or four years, their spirits can droop like their ship's own sails. When they're bored, men are at their most dangerous."

He grew thoughtful, and as I waited for him to continue, I opened a folded copy of the *Tribune* someone had left and let my eyes fall where they might. Illuminated by a nearby gaslight, I read:

BANKRUPT STORE.

No. 81 William Street.
All kinds of Lace and White & Colored
Embroideries cheaper than any other house in the country.
Large line of Carpets & Oilcloths at less than
manufacturer's cost.
Calicoes & Lawn Remnants at 3 cents per yard.

S. SHIREK.

"Do you believe in God?" asked Melville, prompted by some private musing. Thoughts lie penned up in a room, clamorous as cattle in a slaughterhouse, wanting to be let out.

Although I was not sure I did believe in Him, I replied, "Yes."

"But does He believe in you?"

I shrugged and, folding the paper, put it in my coat pocket. I waited for him to say more, but he had lapsed into the silence, which for him was habitual.

"What made you miserable?" I asked, barely concealing my impatience.

At the time, I didn't know that his son Malcolm had shot himself in 1867, that Melville was considered another author whose mature work had failed to live up to its youthful promise, and that he felt like a shipwrecked sailor in the Land of Nod. I had mistaken a melancholia as profound as Edgar Poe's for sullenness. I regretted having agreed to dine with him. A greasy chop and a glass of porter would have been preferable to what now seemed like an inquisition by an inquisitor too weary or withdrawn to question me. I wished that I were elsewhere instead of feeling that I had gone to sleep and awakened inside a gloomy novel set on the English moors.

Unseen within the leafing branches of a poplar tree, a squirrel began to chitter at the approach, no doubt, of a predator with a taste for squirrel. "Cannibalism is more common than the world supposes," I'd heard Melville mutter, upon hearing that a stevedore on the Pearl Street Pier had killed a merchant seaman in a fight over a negro woman and would shortly go to Sing Sing for it. "What is cannibalism if not the spilling of blood to satisfy appetite?" In the animal kingdom, one species serves as another's supper. According to Charles Darwin, it must be so.

Am I being obvious?

I'll tell you what I think, Roebling: The obvious is what, in time, becomes unseen, like a crack in the sidewalk on which one walks each day or a mole on the cheek of someone kissed every morning and night. The obvious can also kill.

Amid the leaves, the squirrel screeched—a weird, unholy sound, which abruptly ceased.

It is a bleak house we live in, and sitting in the park while the first shadows began their sly encroachment on the daylit world, I shivered as if with cold.

"You'll want a drink," said Melville, with something like sympathy in his voice. "And Lizzie will have supper waiting. She's just back from Orange, after seeing to our Fanny's baby."

Waiting, waiting, waiting! The world is consumed by waiting. For the ship to come in, for the tide to go out, for opportunity to knock, for a rich old man to die, for a child to be born, for peace or the outbreak of war, for death or the raising of the dead. The squirrel hidden in the poplar tree cried out in panic, and I grew sad, as if, sitting beside Melville, I had caught his soul's disease.

I followed him through the park and on to Twenty-sixth Street, in which his house stood.

ELIZABETH MELVILLE SHOULD HAVE BEEN HAPPY, but as we sat at the dining table, eating boiled potatoes, green beans, and what—when quick—had been one of the more loathsome parts of a pig, I saw that she was a harried and belittled soul. By the time we had started on the pudding, I'd come to pity her. Despite her seeming abasement, her face—broad and pleasingly arranged—had a formidable aspect even in her middle age. One eye seemed almost closed, as though sight had become oppressive; however, the other eye confronted the world with surety, even defiance. The meal finished, Melville smoked a cigar, his long, square-cut beard trailing in his dirty plate as his head became heavy with drink. I admit to having felt disgust for him, but her admiration was apparent.

Lizzie, as he called her, made polite inquiries concerning my rooming house—the view from the window, the color of the paint, the pattern on the washbowl, the state of the carpet and the bedclothes, the quality of Mrs. McFadden's cooking, the size of the dining table—as well as my pastimes and amusements. Did I enjoy good music, and, if so, had I attended the New York Symphony Society's performance of "Mignon's Lied," by Franz Liszt? Lizzie had not, I suspected. I doubted there was money for such treats in the Melville household. Did I care for contemporary art? What did I think of Winslow Homer? She had read of the recent exhibition of his English watercolors at the Metropolitan. She'd seen a reproduction of one that pictured a young woman, her face hidden by her hair as she leans forward to wring out her dress. Her legs are naked to her knees. A frightened dog is about to flinch, as if at a threat we cannot see.

"I must say, Mr. Ross, I thought the forceful way Mr. Homer painted the headland behind the little group of bathers was grand!"

Melville grunted. "Not half so grand as the sight of a Tahitian girl showing her brown breasts as you would two loaves of bread."

"I wouldn't know about that, Herman," she said drily.

"Along with courthouse hacks and Calvinists, we in the Customs Service share the conviction that man is conceived in sin. Am I not right, Shelby?"

"My husband is fond of startling people with his opinions. But perhaps you've found that out for yourself, Mr. Ross. Is that an English name?"

"My mother came from London, my father from Manchester," I replied.

"One of my ancestors was Abraham—"

"Not to be confused with the patriarch out of Noah," interjected Melville.

"—Shaw."

"Noah was a poor seaman, but an able shipwright."

"Abraham Shaw was born in Yorkshire and settled in the Massachusetts Bay Colony."

"Lizzie refused to be born unless she could claim descent from a citizen of the British Isles. They have their man-eaters, as well, my dear, although they dress in evening clothes."

"My father was a judge," she said, ignoring her husband's gibe.

"Lemuel Shaw, a chief justice of the Massachusetts Supreme Judicial Court, who in his day outraged the abolitionists by returning a runaway slave to his 'ol' massa.'"

He was openly taunting her now, and I marveled that she didn't pick up the platter of congealed fat and bone and bring it crashing down on his head.

"Herman is indebted to my father," she said, as if her prickly husband were in Tahiti or Timbuktu instead of sitting at the table with her in a cramped and drafty house near Kips Bay.

"Mine died raving and insolvent. My grandfather Thomas Melvill, however, dressed up one night as a Red Indian and dumped British tea into Boston Harbor. 'Rally, Mohawks! Bring your axes, and tell King George we'll pay no taxes!' A Freemason and a patriot, he was a friend of Samuel Adams, was present at the 'shot heard round the world,' and had his likeness painted by Copley. To be painted by Mr. Copley is to be granted immortality, according to his admirers. I had *my* portrait done by Asa W. Twitchell, the Lansingburgh wheelwright. I'm not so assured of eternal life as my grandfather, who is presently enjoying his."

He ran his greasy fingers through his hair and continued his sketch of the family tree.

"My maternal grandfather, Colonel Peter Gansevoort, scorched several Mohawk villages—a deed celebrated by my illustrious, if sanguinary, family. The colonel kept slaves, you know—Sambo, Jude, and her two children."

"I'm sure they were well treated, Herman," said Lizzie. If she had intended sarcasm, it went undetected, at least by me. "We have a fine and honorable ancestry."

"Oh, for Christ's sake, Lizzie! Our fancy pedigree has done us no good at all."

"You're not in the forecastle now, Herman, and I'd be wonderfully obliged if you would save your oaths and blasphemies for the barroom. And whatever you may think of our families, you're in their debt, whether you choose to acknowledge the fact or not."

At that moment, Lizzie was magnificent—worthy of the eminent judge who had sired her and a match for the man she had married. I sensed that she had grown impatient long ago with his complaint concerning genius and thwarted destiny.

"You have done a great many things in your life, Herman," she said sternly. I was left unsure whether she had meant to reproach him for a past waywardness or to recognize the tenacity of his struggle with his demons.

He gave her a most peculiar smile, as though inviting—no, challenging her—to go on.

"You earned an engineering degree."

"And never built so much as a privy afterward!"

Unlike you, Roebling, who'll be remembered long after Melville has been forgotten.

"You were a teacher."

"I'd have done better feeding my crumbs of knowledge to the ducks rather than to those hellions."

"You fathered four children—"

"One of whom died."

In that very house on East Twenty-sixth Street.

"—and you wrote books."

"Which the majority of reviewers chewed to pieces and spat out!"

He had recited the history of the family's misfortunes. Whether it was to punish her or himself or to embarrass me, I couldn't have said. Perhaps it was only the bleak, sad story of a life spent together, which husbands and wives will sometimes tell each other before falling to sleep. "We're neglecting out guest."

"Oh, Shelby doesn't mind. He's also a man who has failed to make good." He turned to me and said in a hushed voice, like one careful of another man's sleep, "They speak of me, when they speak of me at all, as the 'buried author.' Shelby understands failure well enough."

I felt a prickling sensation on the skin of my neck, as if chafed by a slowly tightening cord.

"I'm sure that isn't so," she said, glancing sympathetically in my direction.

"What did you do today, Lizzie, while Shelby and I were at Delmonico's, drinking claret with a pinch of ambergris for spice, together with President Chester Arthur, who as collector of the Port of New York enriched himself beyond the dreams of avarice—or what passes for them in the civil service?"

"I blacked the stove, swept the house from top to bottom, and did the shopping for tonight's dinner." She had replied simply to Melville's hectoring and not like a woman with a grievance.

"A veritable feast!" he cried, smacking the table with the flat of his hand.

"It was very tasty, Mrs. Melville," I said. The supper had been peppered and embittered by her husband's black mood. I hoped to propitiate her before Melville's goading brought her to a boil.

"Let's drink a toast to the ragged heart of men. 'Men hunt men as beasts of prey, in the woods and on the way.'"

"Is that one of your verses, Herman?" she asked. "I'm not familiar with it."

He scowled and then said jovially, "'Mrs. Cratchit'! Fetch a bottle of Madeira. Mr. Ross and I intend to drink a toast in honor of the Feast Day of the Cannibals, for surely this is it."

Sighing without ostentation, Lizzie got a bottle of cheap whiskey from the cupboard and set it, together with two small glasses, on the table.

"Never mind those," said Melville, tossing the remains of his beer "down his neck," as the ruffians on the docks like to say.

"What're you waiting for, Shelby?" he asked, wiping his mouth on the back of his hand. "Drink up!"

I drank the rest of my beer in a single gulp and belched.

"Coarse manners for an erstwhile merchant prince of New York!" He filled the glasses webbed by "Belgian lace" with whiskey and slapped the table once again. "We'll drink till our backstays snap and we're dismasted."

"Mind your nerves don't come undone," said Lizzie with gentle admonition.

Melville ignored her. "To cannibals everywhere! Because who is there who is not one?"

"Well, I'm sure *I'm* not," said Lizzie. "I can hardly stand at the butcher's counter without growing faint at the sight of his apron spattered with blood."

"To anthropophagy!" shouted Melville, who'd soon be staggering over words of more than two syllables.

"To the Donner Party!" I cried, having entered a kind of maelstrom stirred by my host's dark enthusiasm.

"To the men of the whale ship *Essex,* who ate one another in their lifeboats!"

"To meat!" I shouted in a rapture that rightly belonged to someone else.

"To the flesh lovers of the world and to their unappeasable appetites!"

He picked up a remnant ham bone from the greasy platter and began to gnaw on it. In disgust, I felt my stomach flip and gripe.

"Cannibalism runs in the blood of mankind," he said almost in a whisper. "A taint more vicious than the Spanish pox. Why did God give us His son to eat and drink? The world baffles me, Shelby—baffles and defeats me!"

By the fourth whiskey, the sweat had come out on Melville's face. He regarded his wife in silence and then said with a cruelty nourished by intoxication, "Lizzie's quite a busy woman. Perhaps not so busy as Washington Roebling's wife, who ever since her husband took sick has been supervising the construction of the world's greatest bridge."

He was speaking with the nonchalance of a tightrope walker, a facility that comes, now and then, to drunkards. I wondered how long he could continue before his sentences fell apart.

"Did you know, Shelby, that Roebling initiated his able lady into arcane matters such as structural analysis, cable construction, and catenary curves? Only the Roeblings and God know what *they* might be."

Elizabeth stood and began to clear the table.

"Let the damn dishes be!"

She did as she was told, her mouth frozen in a tight-lipped smile.

"Think of it, Shelby! Today while Lizzie was blackening the stove, Mrs. Roebling was calculating catenary curves! Naturally, I wasn't there to see her. I must take it on trust and without the evidence of my eyes, which are, in any case, bad. I was in our money pit, as well as in and out of the holds of sailing ships, which—in my dreams—could carry me to the China Sea or the Galápagos, where emperor penguins feed on little fish. In actuality, the *Panama* had just arrived with potash from Liverpool, and the *Vlissingen* with salted herring from Vlissingen. You can smell them on my hand."

He thrust it under my nose so that I could verify the piquant fact, although I had only to sniff my own, which stank of fish, regardless of the scrubbing I'd given them.

"What great novels will be written about such inglorious voyages and cargos of herring and potash?" he asked. "None fit to print except in the shipping news!" Gazing into his glass, as if he might discover the future there, he grew thoughtful and said, "Commerce has always been an enemy of literature, and the writer forced to rely on patronage, even if his name was William Shakespeare. Let's drink to *him*."

"To Shakespeare!" I cried. By this time, the drunken boat was making for the blessed isles of forgetfulness.

"Tomorrow being Sunday and a day of rest, you, Mr. Ross, will accompany me to church." Looking defiantly into Lizzie's eyes, which did not waver, Melville tore a button from his shirt. "My shirt seems to have lost a button."

"I'll sew it back on before you leave tomorrow," she said impassively.

"Thank you, my dear. I wouldn't dream of venturing into the house of the Lord dressed like a sloven or a beggar. Think of it, Shelby! Young ladies used to come near to swooning at the sight of me! I was a handsome, virile, rough-and-ready fellow after four years at sea! Why, at a ball at the Russian embassy, I succeeded in fascinating one of the prettiest girls in Bond Street!" His voice had rung out merrily, his subsequent defeat momentarily forgotten.

"You've had enough to drink for one night, Herman," she said, her eyes boring into his.

"Bollocks!" he grunted, turning away from her.

"When he was a younger man, Herman lost his wits," she said, as if it had been a box of toy soldiers that had gone missing. "Until they returned, I was frightened for the children."

"Yes, I came close to wearing a camisole," he replied with an inscrutable smile.

"He's much better now that he no longer tortures himself by writing novels." She took the glass from his hand and delivered the coup de grâce matter-of-factly: "Which nobody reads."

It was the first I'd heard of Melville the novelist.

He sank back in his chair and said, "Don't think for a moment, Shelby, that I pity myself any more than a whale does for having its back turned into a pincushion. It feels only an anger as large as the universe."

He pushed back his chair and staggered upstairs to bed.

I stood and instantly sat down again, too drunk to walk.

"You can sleep on the sofa, Mr. Ross."

Again, I attempted to get to my feet, but I'd completely lost my bearings now that the compass needle inside my head was swinging crazily.

"I should not try it if I were you," she said gently. "Herman is not always this way. He shouldn't drink, you know, and for the most part, he is careful."

She helped me into the other room and onto a shabby sofa. Trying to kiss her hand in gratitude for her kindness, I kissed my own instead. She left and appeared again with a blanket and a tatty-looking pillow needlepointed with the image of the great whale Moby Dick, which she had made for Melville at the peak of his writing career, before it was his turn to tumble down into obscurity. She quenched the lights efficiently and went upstairs to join her husband, leaving me to turn in a fitful sleep, like a dolphin gamboling in the sea. I remember having dreamed that I was sick, and when I awoke sometime in the night, I touched my beard and the blanket under my chin, afraid that I'd vomited on myself. I was glad to find that I had not, although my head still spun and my gut twisted in dry spasms.

It was then that I heard a voice speaking low, as if to a child weeping inconsolably in the night. I strained to hear while the voice went on softly. In time, the crying became less, until it ceased altogether, and then I heard Elizabeth say, "It's all right, Herman. You mustn't torment yourself." Melville muttered something I did not catch. "I understand," she replied, "although you do sometimes make my life a misery."

"I'm a brute!" he replied, his voice rising, so that I could hear it without needing to hold my breath. "I should have died outright the day Joe Smith's horse bolted on the way to Backus block."

"You mustn't say that."

"Why? Will God strike me dead with a bolt of lightning? I'd rather that than a harpoon with an iron head. Poor beasts!"

"Close your eyes, Herman."

"I miss our farm in Pittsfield, Lizzie. We were happy then, when Hawthorne was among us. The fire's out."

"Shall I sing you to sleep?"

"Yes, please!" He sounded as eager and grateful as a boy accepting a currant bun.

Elizabeth began to sing, but her voice would sometimes fall away, as if the wind had snatched it from her lips.

> Come shake your dull Noddles, ye Pumpkins,
>   and bawl,
> And own you are. . . .
> In Folly you're born, and in Folly you'll live . . .

The song ended, and silence returned to the room upstairs. My eyes having been wide open, I could make out, here and there, certain objects in the darkness by the little light that fell through the curtained window. On the wall above the hearth was a large picture, which I'd only glanced at as I walked through the sitting room into the dining room. It was, I recalled, an oil painting of a coastal schooner endangered by a rocky headland. On the wall opposite, a musket rested on two brackets. I wondered if it had once belonged to Thomas

Melvill, who might have shouldered it on North Bridge against the redcoats. Melville's rolltop desk sat hunched in a corner with the sullen mystery of a dwarf. Next to it was the cabinet in which the works of his friend Hawthorne rested in state. I swear to you, Roebling, that a ray of light was falling onto his likeness burned onto an ambrotype, as implausibly as though I were not in a room on East Twenty-sixth Street, but one in a gothic novel by Ann Radcliffe.

I recall nothing more of that night until I was awakened by Melville at eight o'clock. He was neatly dressed in a black sackcloth coat and trousers, a shirt—with all its buttons— and a clean starched collar. He gestured toward a chair and said that Lizzie had aired and brushed my clothes.

"Come into the dining room when you're dressed. Lizzie made us a breakfast fit for an admiral. She awoke at six bells and went to the butcher's for a piece of gammon."

My nostrils flared involuntarily as I took in the incomparable odors of coffee, fried ham and potatoes. I dressed and polished my boots on the blanket's satin hem. Recalling the misery of the night, I thought I was entitled to the liberty.

At the table, I hesitated to begin on the meat and potatoes, afraid my gorge would rise, but only for a moment. The bile and sway of a landsman's version of seasickness had passed.

"Lizzie's gone to church with a friend. She said to tell you good-bye and that you must come again when we're more ourselves."

I promised myself that I would not endure another such night. Melville was all smiles and pleasantries, however, and I began to doubt my recollection of the ghastly supper and of having overheard his childish tears. I'd drunk a good deal of whiskey—more than I could hold—and possibly my memory was colored by distemper. Memory is a tattered cloth, full of holes and little better than a rag to clean away the dust laid down by time. Little by little, I began to warm to Melville as I had not done during the three months I'd known him.

He's not a bad sort, I said to myself. It's not easy to be brave when the cards turn against you, and much that passes for bravery among us is mere bravado. I haven't always acquitted myself with dignity after fortune no longer smiled.

"Shall we go and pay our respects to the Almighty?" he asked.

St. Paul's Chapel at 209 Broadway, Lower Manhattan, April 16, 1882

Melville and I walked to Union Square, where we boarded a southbound Bowery-Harlem car. The day was fine, the clear sky one that would have given Thoreau or Whitman fits of ecstasy. The elms, buttonwoods, poplars, and chestnuts on either side of the thoroughfare shone with the polished brightwork of new leaves. The car rocked on its springs as the locomotive tugged it over the rails, and I gave myself up to the sights and sounds of the city on the Sabbath and to the tonic river smell stirred by a quickening breeze. We were soon rid of whatever vapors had been left us by the night's debauch. Melville was cheerful—even charming—and I was glad to be in his company. The traffic moved leisurely, but the pavements were jammed with people, their state of grace or the errors of their way concealed beneath Sunday finery.

The vicious and the drunks who had not perished during the night were asleep in their beds or in some filthy alley. Everywhere bells rang out a time different from those tolling wearily for sailors aboard ships headed for Patagonia, Zanzibar—or Red Hook, where the Stony Creek granite blocks for your bridge had once been stored. What dank mineral dreams had been theirs? I wonder. And will they come to dream of something rapturous in their aerie above the slate gray river?

We got off the train at City Hall Park and walked down Broadway to Cortlandt Street—two blocks south of Fulton and four blocks north of Wall Street and the U.S. Custom House. We went along Cortlandt until we came to a house at number fifty-five.

"When I was a very young boy, I lived here, together with my brothers, Gansevoort and Allan, and my sisters Helen and Augusta," he said. "I would listen to my Gansevoort relations and my father's merchant friends tell old Dutch tales of Batavia, called "*Het kerkhof der Europeanen*," the cemetery of the Europeans, of *Chinezenmoord*, the murder of ten thousand Chinese, and of the Java War, which followed. I heard stories of the mutiny at Mindanao; of New Guinea, Shark Bay, and Arnhem Land; of Rottenest, named for the multitude of rats' nests found on the island; of Mauritius and India; of smallpox, measles, and fevers more fatal to the natives than an army of Dutch soldiers. Father's visitors would smoke clay pipes with the stolid self-importance of burghers or drink Holland gin as though they were sitting in their fathers' or grandfathers' houses in Amsterdam or Leyden, warming themselves at a hearth tiled in blue-and-white Delft. They would dream of exploration and conquest, commercial rivalries, treason and betrayals, the black swans of Australia, the rara avises, of gum trees, parrots, nautilus shells like Gothic turrets hiding a tiny Minotaur, and the exotic *bêche-de-mer,* a delicacy for the Chinese, though inedible to the Dutch.

"In this house, my sister and I came down with scarlet fever. No, I'm wrong. That was just after our remove to Bleecker Street. My hearing was never the same again, and even now I enter a kind of twilight of sound, which muffles the world, as though my ears were packed with flannel or musket wadding."

"Were you happy as a child?"

"I would like to think so," he replied equivocally.

I let it go. A man's childhood is his own business, so, too, his marriage. I glanced sharply at Melville, and for an instant, I thought I could see a boy terrified inside the man. The sound of his weeping during the night came to mind, and I felt sorry for him.

He took my arm and led me up Broadway to Fulton and Vesey streets, where St. Paul's Chapel stands. A statue of the apostle, roughly carved in oak, overlooks the busy road from its niche beneath a gable roof.

Roebling, you don't need me to remind you of our city's monuments. According to the *Times,* your bridge will stand among the greatest of any devoted to "the secular ideal."

Just as we arrived, a young man was going in at the church door. I thought I recognized him as one of the weighers on Gansevoort Pier.

"Isn't that Martin Finch?" I asked.

"That's he. He sings in the choir. He has a voice that hasn't broken for all his twenty years and won't break glass like a castrato's, whose manhood was taken by the goddamn priests. Voice like a lark. I heard it once while I was standing here and debating with myself whether I ought to go inside. He's a timid sort, not what we're used to on the docks. But he's honest and, unlike some I could name, civil."

I knew he meant John Gibbs, who had been several times admonished for his insolence.

"Gibbs knows his business, I'll say that much, or I'd have had his bollocks long ago."

"He's a brute," I said absently.

"His face looks as if it'd been holystoned, and he's got the telltale nose of a boozer."

I made a guttural noise, signifying both assent and attentiveness, but Melville made no additional comment.

On several occasions, I had spoken to Martin Finch and thought him agreeable and uncommonly frank. He liked, he'd said, to look at pictures and to attend, whenever he could, musical evenings or lectures at the lyceums in Brooklyn and on Staten Island. Although few men would have thought it worth the waste of breath, he had boasted of having heard Emerson deliver an address at the Cooper Institute called the "Conduct of Life," and, afterward, of having shaken hands with his idol. Martin also admitted shyly that he read verse, especially that by Swinburne and the Rossettis. These pastimes constituted his secret world, which he hid even from his brother, although they shared a small house in

Maiden Lane, not far from St. Paul's. I wondered that such a bright and winning creature could brave the shadows and pestilential curses of "Sailors Town." I wondered even more that he had chosen to show me, a stranger, the gentle aspect of his character. Had I been a man like John Gibbs, his life would have been henceforth hell's own misery and torment. Gibbs would have picked him clean of his angelic pinfeathers and then roasted him alive.

Meanwhile, Melville had, in a manner of speaking, lain abaft the church door. "I seldom go inside," he confided. "The Calvinism I was made to swallow acted on me like an emetic or like the castor oil Miss Watson spooned down Huck Finn's gullet. It wrung me dry of faith."

He leaned against a black iron railing enclosing the chapel cemetery.

"Backward and forward, eternity is the same; already we have been the nothing we dread to be."

The church bell began to toll, as though in mourning for us all.

A young married couple—he, dressed in a stovepipe hat and white bow tie at his winged collar, she, a pretty thing, in a long jacket and skirt, which she had boldly shed of her mother's bustle—looked askance at us as they hurried into church.

According to my watch, it had gone ten o'clock, and in a moment, the morning hymn was taken up by those inside. I pictured the young woman, her hat perched jauntily on her pretty head, and Martin Finch, his clear voice ascending toward his God, like smoke from an offering—incense coiling upward from the priest's gold thurible. Melville seemed to have forgotten our purpose in coming to the chapel. He spoke like a curator or guide conducting a walking tour of lower Manhattan.

"The Chapel used to be Anglican when the British were masters here—a faith as far removed from the Dutch Reformed Church of my father as the North Pole is from the South." He lit a cigar, which seemed irreligious on the Sabbath, when the priest's solemn voice could be heard through the windows. "They call it a 'chapel of ease.' Sailors come here—those who haven't gone to the devil—who wouldn't set foot in Trinity Church or other fancy palace of worship. The chapel is what passes in Manhattan for the Seamen's Bethel, the whalers' church in New Bedford."

I let him talk, not caring if we spent the hour in the fresh air of Broadway instead of the stale air and staler sentiments I imagined were putting the congregation to sleep on a warm April day.

"George Washington prayed here when New York was the capital city. I can imagine him tortured by self-doubt like any other man, on his knees, bargaining with the Almighty. In the end, the world is arranged according to the laws of business and the principle of the survival of the fittest." He spat a loose tobacco shred onto the pavement and concluded by saying, "Dog does not eat dog, but men will when they're hungry."

A lumbering wagon jolting over the cobblestones awoke Melville from his reverie. The teamster cracked his whip over the backs of the poor beasts and shouted a tremendous oath into the sedate street. The congregation seemed to reply with the singing of a hymn, whose words I could not catch.

"It hurts no one—not even me—to come here on occasion and sing the old hymns," said Melville. He sang a few verses from one of the Psalms—for my benefit, as I supposed.

> For the Lord is a great God, and a great King
>   above all gods.
> In his hand are the deep places of the earth:
>   the strength of the hills is his also.
> The sea is his, and he made it: and his hands
>   formed the dry land.

"Are you a religious man, Shelby?"

"Not especially."

"God and I have agreed to ignore each other. I hope never to backslide into religious mania, which can turn a man's wits as readily as gin. The spirit in the bottle—Jinn or distilled grain—is all a man needs for consolation."

"I can't make out whether you're a Christian or—"

"An infidel?" He spoke now like a boy who had behaved naughtily and wanted the world to know it.

"An unbeliever," I replied.

"I don't think God particularly wants our adoration, or our fear, either."

"What then?"

"Maybe He wants our sympathy or our forgiveness for having made us so inadequately. If we are, as is said, fashioned in His likeness, He must be a curious deity—perhaps a helpless one. Or like Hephaestus, a lame and imperfect god. He might, as literary critics put it, have only limited omniscience. In this, He would be only slightly better off than His creatures."

"It's too late to go inside," I said, showing him the time as it is kept by men.

"What do you say we take a look at Roebling's bridge? I'd like to assure myself it is there; that it hasn't been an illusion meant to deceive us into thinking we are masters of the universe."

"Do you believe in anything, Herman?"

"Yes. It's better to sleep with a sober cannibal than a drunken Christian."

WE WALKED ON BEEKMAN TOWARD PECK SLIP. The day might have belonged to God elsewhere in the city, but here, amid warehouses and foundries, the streets were noisy with the ruck and riot of men whose house of worship had moist sawdust on the floor and a dented spittoon instead of a collection plate. We stopped to buy oysters from a man whose face looked like weathered stone and whose gnarled fingers bore the scars of his trade. We ate them off newspapers that had, like the oysters, been fresh the previous day. Mine, the *Brooklyn Eagle*, carried a story concerning an architect named William Graul, "Accused of Taking Bribes." The front page of the *New-York Tribune* wrapping Melville's oysters included a curious notice regarding the "grave of serious literature," as Melville called it after having read it aloud.

LITERATURE AS A LAST RESORT.

Among the unredeemed pledges exposed in a city pawnshop window, books of a religious nature (the Bible, "Lives of the Saints," &c.) are predominant. Dictionaries stand next in order, followed by works of the modern novelists.

"Lizzie uses Noah Webster as a doorstop when the house is drafty."

She could use his dictionary as a footstool or a chopping block, for all I cared. The river's damp was getting in my bones. The April sun didn't warm those narrow streets packed with brick buildings put up during the war for the manufacture of tinware, iron chests, steam engines, rifle barrels, and barrel staves. Paint scaling, fixtures rusting, bricks in need of pointing, and, here and there, a window of glazing, the old buildings—along with their owners—had not recovered from the depression. As if in mourning for the useful past, an east wind was blowing chill ocean air into Peck Street, augmenting the briny smell of the remaining oysters in our laps. I imagined the wind playing an adagio on the harp strings of the gigantic bridge, which loomed above the rooftops.

"It's a saurian monster about to climb out of the river and trample the city underfoot," said Melville. "Who would have thought that mere men could have raised such a colossus?"

We boarded a steam ferry for Brooklyn. Melville appeared

to be moved by the familiar scene, a miniature voyage drained of color, interest, and certainly romance. Watching the approach of the sprawling Grand Ferry Terminal, a Carpenter Gothic heap of wooden turrets and spires, fancy scrollwork, arcades, and a rooftop promenade, at the foot of Brooklyn's Fulton Street, he muttered a few lines of verse to himself or to the choppy water lapping at the hull.

> Passage to India!
> Lo, soul! seest thou not God's purpose from the
>   first?
> The earth to be spann'd, connected by network,
> The races, neighbors, to marry and be given in
>   marriage,
> The oceans to be cross'd, the distant brought near,
> The lands to be welded together.

"Walt wrote those lines to celebrate the opening of the Suez Canal in '69, the year the first transcontinental railroad was finished. I wonder what he really thinks of all *this*?" With a sweep of his arm, Melville embraced the monumental towers strung with enough steel cables to reach Australia. "The bridge must wait, I think, for a poet of the future to sing its praises."

Sad to think Walt Whitman will never see your bridge finished, Roebling—now that a stroke has left him housebound in Camden. You have that in common, if nothing else.

"The roadway is a mile long," I said, descending into bathos, like the American eagle hauled down from the empyrean and stamped onto a quarter-dollar piece. Thus is spirit ever debased by commerce, Melville would have said. If he'd been lucky in his art, he'd probably have whistled a different tune.

I recited the weights and measures of your prodigy, Roebling, as if I were inspecting a cargo of mullet.

Ignoring my prosaic remarks, Melville said, "The bridge is important as a secular symbol of ascension and as potent as the Trinity Church steeple, which must humble itself before this feat of engineering—a sure sign that industry and not faith are uppermost in the modern mind."

No longer the tallest structure in Manhattan, the steeple rose like a needle above the land receding behind us as the ferryboat drew Brooklyn ever nearer. To be on a boat in motion is to understand illusion. To recall that the Earth is also in motion is to understand our bewilderment before God, who, Melville, in one of his black moods, said is either a deaf-mute or a gibbering maniac.

Steam tugs, barges, hay boats, lighters, sailing ships, and packets mobbing the lower river yielded to our passage like courtiers at a royal progress or simpering civil servants.

"Whitman probably considers the bridge to be the death of something fine. The America he knows and loves, which, like the world of Cooper's Indians or Irving's comical Dutchmen, is fated to pass away. If it ever really existed." He chewed a ragged nail, then said, "It's as if a laundry boiler were soon to replace the *Argo* and a gaggle of Chinamen Jason's Argonauts."

The ferry whistle hooted in derision, and our boat having

slowed, the Brooklyn depot jumped up quickly before us. He grew somber as its immense shadow fell over him, and then he said, "Why don't we pay Washington Roebling a visit and hear what the chief engineer has to say on the subject? His opinion of the bridge's future is bound to be sanguine, and, therefore, will be an antidote to my gloom."

"I read that he seldom sees anyone."

"His nervous constitution was ruined by caisson disease, but he's not the crippled invalid and recluse most suppose."

Forgive me, Roebling; I get so engrossed in my tales, I sometimes forget to whom I'm speaking. You're not finding it tedious? Would you like me to stop? . . . Then I'll keep talking until you tire of me and my jawing. If you fall asleep, I'll talk to that fly crawling on that crust of bread. I wonder if it also feels its smallness in the scale of creation, or does it believe itself to be a god.

"But will he see us?" I asked Melville, as we started toward the bluffs, which rise above the river on the Brooklyn side.

"It's true he sees very few people unconnected with the work and refuses interviews. We have nothing to lose, however, but a little time, since we're already here. His house is up there on the heights. You can see his window glaring in the afternoon sun. The view of the bridge from his second-story room must be spectacular."

We walked along Columbia Heights to the brownstone at number 110.

Roebling's Second-Story Room on Brooklyn Heights, April 16, 1882

That afternoon on Brooklyn Heights, I didn't tell Melville that you and I had known each other. Perhaps I was afraid you would choose not to see me—not because of your sickness, but because you might have heard of my disgrace. You have made something of your life, while I—well, as you can see.

Do you recall the time before the war when our fathers had business dealings? Mine owned a factory that fabricated iron fittings to your father's specifications. It's unlikely you remember our having played "'Priest' Vallon" and "Bill the Butcher" in the factory yard. Your life's been crowded with schools, engineering projects, and the war. I read that you'd been breveted a colonel for bravery at Chancellorsville. Having little of my own, I admire those who do.

Do you remember the winter of 1867, when the river froze? You can't have forgotten it. The ferries were icebound—a situation that made it obvious to those who had fought against it that an East River Bridge was needed. New York City and Brooklyn were cut off from each other unless one were brave enough to walk across the frozen river. Do you remember the day we skated from Fulton Street, Manhattan, to Fulton Street, Brooklyn? I was twenty-four; you would have been twenty-nine, or thirty. I was enrolled at Manhattan College and studying in a desultory way. Unlike you, I had no clear end in view, no aim or ambition except that I wished to get on in life. I wanted to earn enough money to own an apartment uptown, dress fashionably, sit behind a fast horse, and fascinate pretty young ladies—the usual occupations of a young man of the Gilded Age. I had no wish to work, make my mark, or form permanent attachments. I gave as much thought to the purchase of a pair of gloves as I did to a point in Blackstone's *Commentaries*. I was more fastidious about the cut of a coat than a Latin conjugation. But that winter afternoon as you and I sped across the river is fixed in my memory, like a photograph of something marvelous.

It was bitter cold, and the wind from the Atlantic ripsawed through us to the bone, no matter that we were dressed as if for an Arctic expedition. The sky was low and white and, together with the ice-clad river, seemed one vast and contiguous nullity except for a bright helter-skelter of jangling sleighs. Our mouths covered by coachmen's scarves, we said little. When we did speak, our words escaped our mouths, like ghosts. Second Bull Run, Antietam, Chancellorsville, the Wilderness, the siege of Petersburg, and Gettysburg were already behind you, as was the Cincinnati-Covington Bridge, which you and your father had built across the Ohio River. You'd married Emily and, together, you had traveled through Europe, where you studied the sickness that, in five years, would strike you down.

I don't recall why you were in Manhattan that day. Your Emily was home in Trenton with your two-month-old boy. Business, no doubt—business, not God or sexual desire, is the prime mover and the decider of fates.

Do you remember how thrilling it was, Roebling? We might've been sightseeing on the moon or a polar ice cap. It was one of those extraordinary moments of clarity when the slate is erased and all we know and think we know are confounded. Perhaps you felt the same when you flew over Lee's army at Chancellorsville in a reconnaissance balloon or went under the river for the first time inside a pinewood "coffin." The shadows on the caisson walls would have seemed to writhe in the eerie light of the calcium lamps. The silence must have been abysmal! You could have heard the sluicing of your heart while the "sandhogs" shoveled what—at any moment—could have become their grave, and yours. "Death is terrible, tho' borne on angels' wings!"

Do you recall the ships and boats frozen at their moorings—hulls like iron or wooden splinters lodged in the river's skin? We had happened upon something otherworldly, like Ahab's White Whale, which surely had been spawned in one of the moon's ancient seas.

Last week when Melville and I came to visit, Emily— protective of your health and well-being—would not let us inside.

"Mrs. Roebling," said Melville, as we stood in the hallway outside your rooms.

"Can I help you?"

You have a grand and formidable wife, Roebling.

"We've come to see the chief engineer," replied Melville, not in the least subdued.

"I'm sorry, but Mr. Roebling is resting. Does he know either of you gentlemen?"

"No, but we would like to congratulate him on the bridge, which, we understand, is in the final stage of construction."

"If you leave your cards, I'll be sure to give them to my husband when he awakes."

Melville gave her his card, and I mine. I got up on my toes and tried to steal a look over his broad shoulders, but I could make out little more in the gloom than a coat tree, an umbrella, and a pair of rubber boots leaning exhaustedly against the wall.

"Herman Melville, the novelist?" she asked after having read his calling card. I suppose that curiosity was struggling against circumspection in her. My card had provoked neither.

"I am the man!" he replied genially. "Or should I plead guilty and offer you my head?"

"My husband reads your novels. He thinks *Moby-Dick* is very fine."

The night before, Lizzie had mentioned Melville's novels. I wondered what they were about and who or what was Moby Dick.

"He'll be sorry to have missed you and happy you called on him," she said to Melville. She scarcely acknowledged my presence.

"This is my associate, Mr. Ross, also of the United States Customs Service. We came out from Manhattan to view the work and thought, as long as we were in Brooklyn, to visit the chief engineer. We regret we won't have the pleasure. Please give him our regards and our hopes for his complete return to health."

She nodded and gently closed the door on us.

"I'm disappointed that we didn't get to see the man

himself," said Melville as we walked back the way we'd come. "She's a handsome woman as well as a capable one."

I admired her broad and genial face, which in her youth would have been pretty. But years of conveying your instructions to the foremen and their questions to you had worn her to the bone. You could see weariness drawn in charcoal strokes around her eyes and at the corners of her mouth. I felt sorry for her, Roebling, and wondered if she believed the bridge is worth the cost that you and she have dearly paid. Perhaps it's enough for her to have helped to rear a prodigy the like of which the world has seldom seen, and it has seen much through its tired old eyes.

"There's an eating house not far from here, which serves German food at a reasonable price. What do you say, Mr. Ross? Shall we have an early supper in Brooklyn?"

Feeling hungry and well-disposed toward Melville, I agreed.

ARRIVING AT THE CORNER of Fulton and Sands streets, we went inside a white-framed tavern named the Schwarzwald, redolent of onions and tobacco smoke. We sat at a table marred by countless arms and elbows belonging to corpulent Herrs and their ample Fraus, steins of lager beer, and china plates, which had been scarred by madly sawing knives and scorched by briar pipes. We ate heartily from a platter heaped with smoked tongue, chops, brown mustard, and dark bread, drank our fill of German beer, and when we were done and nearly dead with eating, we sat back heavily in our ancient chairs and groaned.

Well-preserved specimens of Herr and Frau crossed the timbered room, their heavy feet shod in brogans, followed by a Fraulein displaying the "Grecian bend"—the old fashioned bearing of ladies obliged to lean forward elegantly, if unnaturally, by their whaleboned clothes. A smart-aleck correspondent at one of the rags had noticed the resemblance of the bend to the bent backs of stricken sandhogs. The name stuck, as names will when set, like barbed hooks, in columns of type to catch the eyes of jaded readers. Thereafter, caisson sickness would be called "the bends."

I know, but I feel as if I were talking to posterity. We're living in an age of marvels—Edison's incandescent bulb, Brunel's colossal ship, *Great Eastern*, Bazalgette's London sewers, the Suez Canal, the transatlantic cable, and now the Brooklyn Bridge—perhaps the greatest of them all. Your bridge, Roebling, now that it is strung and tuned, seems shaped for transmitting voices down through ages hence and, further still, into the ear of God. Is it really so far-fetched when a voice can be laid down on a waxed cylinder and played back a year, ten years—who knows—a century later? And that cylinder is made of cardboard and not fifteen thousand tons of wire and stone! In a time like ours, when the most startling notions become commonplace, fancies are no longer necessarily follies.

Melville nudged me with his foot and asked, "Would you care to stick your harpoon in that girl's bustle?" I attributed his coarseness to the beer, whose foam was still clinging to his mustache.

"She's not my ideal," I replied, my face warming in a blush.

"And what might your ideal woman be?"

"One not partial to pigs' feet and dumplings."

Melville smiled peculiarly. Who can guess what goes on in that brain of his, whose color, if we were to peek inside, would be black like a flag of lost hope. And then he began to laugh deeply, so that his eyes disappeared behind his cheekbones.

"I feel my old good humor returning," he said, picking up his beer stein, shaped like the head of a man, complete with a burgher's mustache and a green alpine hat topped with a feather plucked, I supposed, from a clay-fired pheasant. A pretty conceit, don't you think, Roebling—or have I belabored the obvious again?

"Are you always unkind to your wife?" I think I meant to antagonize him the way a man, even a small man, will sometimes provoke another when his better sense yields to recklessness. "I was embarrassed for her last night."

If a man could—in an instant—change into a beast, Melville did before my eyes.

"Shut your pan, cunt!"

His words both frightened and thrilled me. I searched my mind for an equally scurrilous riposte, but I could think of nothing more insulting than "you scalawag prick!"

He glared and then suddenly laughed. "Shelby, you're quite a desperado!"

I expect that I appeared ashamed by my impertinence

and my insult, however laughable, because he softened toward me.

"You ought to know better than interfere in something that's none of your concern. I've known men to have their ears cut off or their nostrils slit for less."

Involuntarily, I touched my ears and nose.

"Lizzie and I rub along well together, although fifteen years ago, she nearly left me." He stood up from his chair. "And there's an end to it! It's time we were getting back to Manhattan, before we grow commodious like these Germans."

During the ferry's return to the Manhattan depot, a man stood at the taffrail. Dressed in a workman's blue serge coat and slouch hat, he was peering through a camera at the Brooklyn tower behind us.

"There's Thomas Edison," said Melville. "Men like him will make the novel seem a paltry thing."

"And what will the future make of this? I wonder."

I meant your bridge; at that moment, I took no interest in Edison and his genius.

"The future will have advanced at such a pace that Roebling's bridge impresses no more than one of Columbus's antique ships—unless the world will have once again slid backward into a dark age, in which the benighted will either worship or fear it."

I thought the latter case the more likely.

"We would do well to remind ourselves that progress marches on hobnailed boots over those who are out of step." I could not decide whether he had spoken with acrimony or regret.

"Herman, what sort of novels do you write?" I asked the question that had been on my mind since his brief exchange of words with Emily.

"Indifferent ones, by all accounts."

He turned his back on me, and in that gesture, I saw his repudiation of the world, which had forgotten him.

Martin Finch's House in Maiden Lane, Lower Manhattan, April 16, 1882

Disembarking at the Fulton Street slip on the Manhattan side of the river, Melville and I parted company. He'd been asked—*commanded* was the word he used—to meet that evening with the collector of customs, who lived in the neighborhood of Gansevoort Pier. He'd been appointed to the sinecure by President Arthur, a plum for his support during the uncertain days when Garfield lay dying in Washington from two bullets fired by the frustrated office seeker Charles Guiteau.

"Caruthers is an old stickleback and a bore to boot, but in the hierarchy of the Customs Service, he is my lord, and I am his vassal. And don't think he lets me forget it! He wants to inveigle Chester Arthur into visiting his old boneyard. That charming crook lined his pockets here. Caruthers wants to be seen shaking the new president's hand. I suppose he hopes some money will stick to it."

Melville and I wished each other good night and went our separate ways. During the ferry ride home, I had been thinking of paying Martin Finch a visit. He lived on Maiden Lane, not far from the Manhattan depot, along with his brother,

Franklin, and a sister-in-law. It isn't late, I told myself while dithering at the curb. It's only gone half-past six, and I did promise Martin I'd visit if I was ever in the neighborhood.

His brother answered my knock and let me inside the house built of brick in the Federal style of the previous century. Its run-down appearance spoke more of the reduced circumstances of the tenants than their neglect. Martin earned even less than I. Franklin worked as a typesetter in Newspaper Row, on Chatham Street. He was a large, burly man with a reddish beard and a straightforward manner. After calling upstairs to Martin, he questioned me briefly, as though I were the subject of a newspaper story. I answered him without resentment because I understood that curiosity was the disease of his tribe—from copyboy to editor in chief. What stories have passed through his ink-stained hands? I asked myself. What manifold experiences might have seeped into his skin and into his blood and marrow, if it were possible for a man to absorb life through his pores, as well as his senses!

Martin came downstairs and gave me his hand in greeting. Compared to his brother's sturdy frame, the younger man's slightness was all the more apparent. I wondered if he'd been a sickly child or had had a difficult time at birth. A man like Martin would not have had the grit, as an infant, to fight his way into being. This, one knew at a glance. He would have to make his way through life by the charity and goodwill of others.

"Hello, Shelby!" he said with a becoming smile. "I see that you've met my brother."

"Yes."

"Mr. Ross and I sometimes work together on Gansevoort Pier," explained Martin. Franklin made a remark I don't recall.

"I'm glad you came," said Martin. "I noticed you and Mr. Melville outside St. Paul's this morning. I looked for you in church, but you seemed not to have gone inside after all."

"It was a whim of Melville's," I said. "We ended up at Roebling's rooming house in Brooklyn Heights."

If Franklin had been a dog, his ears would have stood up on hearing your name.

"Did you see him?" he asked eagerly.

I told him we hadn't, and his disappointment was evident. "Many believe Roebling is a complete invalid, deprived of the use of his limbs and speech."

Many also think you're a "complete idiot"? Well, there's no shortage of cynical and mean-spirited people abroad in the world. Pygmies will always outnumber giants.

Martin and I strolled down Broadway toward the Battery. We spoke of this and that, as people do whose purpose in conversation is not so much an exchange of opinions as of feelings. I was amazed by how readily the other man was able to draw me out and might have resented it had the evening not been so pleasant.

We stopped in Pearl Street to watch workmen at the Edison Illumination Company's new generating station. Although it was Sunday night, they were busily unloading machinery from a wagon emblazoned with PORTER-ALLEN ENGINE CO., manufacturers of the steam engines that would drive the dynamos. The indefatigable Edison was calmly directing the work. He had on the blue serge jacket, disreputable-looking shoes, and slouch hat he'd worn on the ferry that afternoon. I was struck by his ordinariness; he didn't look like a man who had already invented the phonograph, multiplexing telegraph, and incandescent lightbulb. You and your father when he was alive resemble the picture in our heads evoked by the phrase "great men of science and technology." Edison might have been mistaken for a night watchman.

The scene fascinated Martin. "Think of it, Shelby! This fall, Edison's machinery will begin to banish darkness from New York City. Someday the entire country will be illuminated. In time, people will forget there ever was such a thing as a pitch-black night."

I considered his remark poetical but replied stolidly, "A pity for Edgar Poe and the storytellers of terror and gloom."

"'It was a dark and stormy night,'" intoned Martin lugubriously.

We continued south on Pearl and into Battery Park, where we beheld the confluence of the Hudson and the East River. A mile out in New York Harbor stood Fort Columbus, where Confederate prisoners had been interned. To the east, the towers of your bridge ascended into "twilight's last gleaming"—to steal from Francis Scott Key, who's well past caring. Do you know the feeling, Roebling, that can come at twilight, when the world seems to hold its breath? Of course you do; your windows face the dying sky. I felt something out of the ordinary stir in me.

"Isn't it sublime?" asked Martin, who also felt it.

Moved by the sight of your handiwork, which God might envy were He imbued with the less honorable of human emotions, I almost said something grand, but I didn't want to appear sensitive. Instead, I concealed my emotions in facts.

"The Brooklyn tower reaches three hundred and sixteen feet above the riverbed; the Manhattan tower, three hundred and forty-nine feet." I was being deliberately pedantic, don't you see.

"But that's not what moves us!" cried Martin, exasperated by my obtuseness.

I persisted in being obnoxious. "The magnitude of its construction is sufficient reason to be amazed."

"I am interested in infinitude, which—"

"The bridge is a convenience!" I said, rudely interrupting him. "Anything else is beside the point."

I had hurt his feelings, and for a time he was silent.

We sat on a low stone wall and looked at the slowly blackening harbor. Martin started chattering again—about what, I couldn't have said. As the sun lowered behind the Staten Island hills, I seemed to fall asleep, yet my eyes took in the flight of a seagull across the harbor—its wings flashing in semaphore a message I couldn't read. At the north end of Governor's Island, the red sandstone walls of Castle Williams took fire before turning black and dead, like a cigar ember dropped into the lightless ocean. You could have persuaded yourself that you'd heard its circular walls hiss in the rushing tide of night.

Martin recovered his childlike sense of wonder. "Isn't it marvelous to be living in an age such as this?"

"Yes," I replied, and to myself, I said, The astrolabe was once considered a marvel, and the wheel before it.

I felt a sudden antagonism toward him. He's hardly more than a boy, I told myself; naïve to a fault and absurdly foolish in his enthusiasm. What am I doing here, sitting on a stone wall, which, since night had come on, had turned cold like a marble grave? I was nearly twice his age, and I had passed through the mill and been ground fine as buffalo bones on their way to fertilize a rich woman's roses. My scorn for the boy passed through me like a chill, and I found myself trembling.

"You're a damned fool!" I shouted at him with enough feeling to make the last of the day's pigeons jump and shrug off to wherever pigeons roost, accompanied by the whirring of their wings.

He turned on me the most appalled face, and—can you believe it?—tears appeared in his eyes. "Did I say something stupid?" he asked. I glowered at him for good measure. "I do tend to get carried away. I beg your pardon, Mr. Ross, if I have said anything amiss."

Roebling, he was sulking like a girl! I wanted to hit him in the worst way. (Is there a best way?)

We sat awhile, my feelings vacillating between pity and contempt. I wished that I had gone home to my room on Christopher Street or accompanied Melville to Caruthers's house. I could not see how to extricate myself. The seat of my trousers seemed glued to the stone wall, the soles of my boots to the gravel strewn at my feet. Night had arrived in earnest, and the Battery was engulfed, except for the gas lamps, which shed a maleficent light onto the paths. The upper-story windows in the Western Union Building flamed briefly in the weakening light before they, too, were quenched.

I had watched the water being drained of color. It had turned turquois, ruby, gold, pearl, lead, and finally jet. What do I care for poetry? I thought. What earthly good is a sensitive soul?

Martin coughed once and then fell silent. I swear, Roebling, if he had snuffled or given license to his tears, I would have killed him. I would have dragged his body to the water's edge and launched it!

If not for John Gibbs, our uneasy vigil might have continued until morning. He had been drinking up his wages in a Fulton Street taproom near the ferry slip—he would later say, gloating over his stealth—when he saw me standing hesitantly on the pavement. Sensing my indecision, he thought it would be good sport to follow me when at last I set out to visit Martin. Seeing the two of us leaving his house together, Gibbs was certain of his prey. Like all of his kind, he has a knack for searching out another's weakness.

As we walked down Broadway and into Pearl, we were stalked with the cunning of Magua, whom the French called "Le Renard Subtil," the wily fox, in Cooper's *The Last of the Mohicans*. Gibbs may be toadlike in appearance, but a reptilian strength lies coiled within him, and he relishes causing others pain. He exults in their misery, as if the musk of their fear were ambergris. He is cruel and, despite his bluster, not a man to take lightly. Whether it was the lengthening shadows in the streets, the craftiness with which he followed us, or our mutual absorption, neither Martin nor I had noticed him—not even when we stopped to watch Edison's men at work on the Pearl Street generating station. Gibbs was there, lurking in an alleyway.

I would not call him "Iago"; Shakespeare's villain was a winning, plausible fellow ostensibly devoted to the Moor. Gibbs is devoted to no one but himself and carries the evidence of his vices as plainly as a venomous snake does its rattle. After the bloody business with the knife in the *Saxony*'s hold, I ought to have been warier.

Because our backs were turned to the city, Gibbs had managed to cross the Negro Burial Ground and the Battery, stealing among the juniper and gooseberry bushes unseen by Martin and me, despite the uncomfortable silence we were keeping. Gibbs appeared with the suddenness of an apparition, ghoulish and foul.

"I see what I see, and I know what I know!" he sneered, his face near enough mine for me to smell a vile stew of onions, beer, whiskey, and cigars on his breath.

Startled, I said nothing, while Martin yelped. Gibbs laid a finger beside his nose and repeated his insinuation, whose meaning was unclear to me. I could see his missing teeth and blackened gums, his split lips, and his bloodshot eyes. His beard was befouled by spittle, ash, and grease. His hand, when he touched my cheek, smelled of oyster brine. Never before had I encountered a more odious human being. He seemed too obvious a villain to exist apart from melodrama, and I have often wondered if he studies the part to produce an effect on his victims.

"Are you boys behaving yourselves?" he asked, his voice sleek and at the same time coarse as a piece of nubby silk.

"What do you want, Gibbs?" I was finally able to ask. I hoped that my voice conveyed defiance and declared my intention not to be cowed. I'm afraid it did neither.

"Nothing, Mr. Ross, nothing at all!" he replied merrily. "I was out walking the dog, when I saw my two friends sitting by themselves and thought the three of us could make a party. But seeing how you're together, enjoying the moon and such, I decided to say hello and then be on my way. I must say, Mr. Ross, your tone isn't friendly; it is, if you want my opinion, offensive. You ought to know better, having been a gentleman, if only of the codfish aristocracy. I'd have thought you'd learned some manners. And you, *Mr.* Finch, what do you have to say for yourself? Shocking piece of rudeness I'd say—your not having the courtesy to acknowledge me! But then you've always been odd—haven't you? Moping about the pier, ogling some book or other! You've the look of a mooncalf, Mr. Finch. Or perhaps you'll allow me the privilege of calling you by your Christian name. What is your given name, *Mr.* Finch?"

Martin mumbled his name.

"What's that?" asked Gibbs, shaping his hand into a hearing trumpet. "You'll have to speak up. I don't hear so well as I used to when I was a boy. It's the goddamn wharf! A noisy, stinking place—don't you fellows find it so? Of course, Shelby has the old man's ear. He's the inspector's pet. Lucky for him. But you, *boy*." He turned to poor Martin again. "You, with the pretty face. You're not under anybody's wing. You could disappear, and nobody'd be the wiser. Your place in the Customs Service is the lowliest of all. First, there's the chief crook, President Chester A. Arthur; then there are the collector of customs for the Port of New York and the naval officer, both of whom excel in graft; next come the surveyor, the deputy surveyor, and our own District Inspector Melville; then we come to Mr. Ross, appraiser, then me, and, finally, we get to you, Martin, *assistant* weigher. At two dollars a day, you're lower than whale shit! Well, I seem to have known your name after all!"

I could hear Martin's muffled groans and felt contemptuous of his lack of manliness. But was that fair? He was out of his element. I doubt there's a man living in the marble houses of Fifth Avenue or Bond and Great Jones streets who could thrash Gibbs, a bully and a brawler. Gentlemen can be brutal, though they conceal the fact beneath their fine clothes and patronage of charity hospitals and opera houses, but they couldn't have stood up to Gibbs, no more than a pedigree dog can fight a tenement rat. Martin might have been poor and plebian, but he hadn't the mean streak of a street ruffian. Emboldened by rage, I struck our tormentor's face. The blow sent him reeling.

"Goddamn it!" he shouted, wiping blood on the back of his hand.

Now it was he who drew a knife. I glared at him; we glared

at each other; and in each other's eyes, there was nothing to see except hatred. We were drawn by the force of its attraction and equally repelled by it like two magnets whirling in one of Edison's dynamos. We wanted to hurl ourselves at each other and simultaneously felt that such an action would be impossible and contrary to some law of the universe governing the interactions of men. The moment passed too quickly for me to have parsed it, nor could I have had a notion of what went on inside Gibbs's mind; the thoughts of a degenerate brain are impossible to guess. Since that night on the Battery, however, I've imagined them as they raced like sharks beneath his consciousness.

Gibbs folded his knife and put it in his pocket, and then he did a most astounding thing: He put his arms around us and, like a father who'd lost his temper over some trifling matter, he apologized first to Martin and then to me.

"I'll say good night," he said, and in a moment, he was gone, leaving us in perplexity.

I didn't feel like talking, and apparently neither did Martin. Without a word, we walked back the way we'd come. I glanced behind me toward the bridge, but there was nothing to be seen of it.

West Street Customs Office, April 17, 1882

"My father sold French silks, Canadian furs, and California ostrich feathers at New York City auction houses, and by his fifties, he managed to ruin himself and his health in spite of his brother-in-law Gansevoort's financial assistance, which, as far as Father could see, had no bottom. He died in '32, a disgraced bankrupt."

Melville was in a talkative mood as we sat eating lunch in our West Street office.

"Bankruptcy is not an exclusive club; it is one to which even *I* used to belong," I said—drolly, I hoped. "If this were one of Dickens's novels"—my hand took in our office and, by extension, the city of New York—"we'd be coughing up blood in the Tombs."

"We're surrounded by the world's riches like two pashas and not a pair of disgruntled, underpaid civil servants," he said, cutting the loaf of dark brown bread he favored. "Awaiting our pleasure, according to the bills of lading, are cotton and perique from St. James Parish, porcelain and silk from Canton, rosewood, mahogany, and teak from Papua, rum from the West Indies, cocoa beans from Maracaibo, sugar and salt from Curaçao, tea and spices from Calcutta, coffee beans from Java, cheeses from Marseilles, fancy lacework from Flanders, and fine linens from Belgium. The world comes to us, Shelby; we've only to sit and wait and, when it arrives, weigh, count, and appraise its commodities. And of course tax them." He divided a sausage with his knife and concluded his paean to international trade: "We're living in a storybook, my friend."

"It gives me small satisfaction to be no more than a conduit through which abundance flows; it might as well be sewage for all the good it does me," I commented rudely.

"When I was a boy, my mother read to me *The Travels of Marco Polo*. My mind was filled with voyages, and my walks with Father and my brother Gansevoort along the piers made my head spin. I longed to be a tattooed sailor. There were plenty of them about to frighten and enthrall a boy whose head was lost in the clouds above Tierra del Fuego and whose young heart beat like a ship's drum calling men to quarters. What a life! I could taste it." He took a bite of bread and another of sausage. "For a while, I lived it and relished every bit of it!" He chewed and swallowed as though he'd bitten off a piece of life itself, substantial as coarse German bread and savory as wurst. "Too soon, I gave it up."

"I wanted to be a merchant prince."

"Why?"

My aspiration appeared to have baffled him. But he might as well have asked a bird why it flies, a worm why it crawls, or a child why he's dying of cholera.

"Why would you have wished for such a small thing? To spend your days in auction houses and countinghouses, in stock exchanges and traders' pits, in bourses and banks, where men always sell themselves short. It was an ignoble dream, Shelby!"

"It was mine and my father's!" I said, annoyed by his rebuke. "We can't all get tattooed, tar our pigtails, and go to sea." Or write books that no one bothers to read, I added silently.

"Shelby, I'm afraid you have no imagination."

"Imagination is not among the qualities of a good businessman, Herman."

During one of our earlier conversations, Martin had said that I had "a poetical strain," an idea that pleased and also frightened me. I would not have wished to look into my glass and see a poet instead of a man. And yet I had once tried to be a gentleman and had purchased the latest works by Elizabeth Browning, Coventry Patmore, and our own John Greenleaf Whittier. (I couldn't stomach Whitman.) Now here I was once more, declaring my mind to be prosaic, as if by undervaluing it, I hoped to pay a lesser tax.

Melville might have retorted that I had shown myself to be a poor businessman, but he said, "In my imagination, earth is covered by ocean." He tapped his temple with a forefinger, a gesture denoting wisdom or madness. "Dry land was one of God's earliest mistakes: He should have stopped at the great whales." He cast an eye on the harpoon leaning against the wall. "I swear there is nothing on this earth so godlike as the sea and that I was never so happy as when I went down to it in ships!"

"The sea is a graveyard, an obstacle to trade, and, at best, a source of food for those who eat mackerel on Fridays," I said, intending to be contrary.

"Spoken like a true landsman," he said, shaking his head in disapproval.

"I *am* a landsman!"

"No need to raise your voice!" he shouted, as if he were on the quarterdeck and I aloft among thunderously flapping sails.

"You seem bent on belittling me today," I retorted, with something like—God help me!—hurt feelings.

"If I have done, I apologize," he said with a charming smile. "Caruthers was Christ's own centurion last night."

I supposed I had given him a look of bafflement, because he clarified his allusion: "The irreligious Roman with the spear. Caruthers seemed to enjoy twisting it between my ribs."

"Will he get what he wants?" Now it was he who was baffled. "Caruthers."

"Once a man has everything he needs, there seems to be nothing to stop him from getting all that he wants."

We fell silent, each entertaining his own thoughts.

"And how was *your* evening?" asked Melville after he had finished his lunch and swept the crumbs from his desk into the palm of his hand.

"Uneventful," I replied, having already decided I would lie to him. "I went home and to bed."

"You're a lucky man. I'd rather have slept with a cannibal than had brandy and cigars with the collector of customs, Herr Caruthers. Havana cigars and French cognac, mind you. The duty on the spirits, I recall, was appraised at eighty cents a gallon. The cigars had been seized as contraband. The big bugs of our service are only slightly less dishonest than was Boss Tweed."

Finding no place more convenient, Melville stowed the bread crumbs in his pocket.

"How is Finch doing?" I asked, and immediately regretted it.

"Finch?"

"Martin Finch." I felt sweat start out on my forehead.

"The slight fellow we saw yesterday going into St. Paul's?"

I nodded.

"I've heard nothing against him." He paused, then said, "You sometimes work together in the holds or in the scale house."

"We do," I replied, as though I'd been found guilty of colluding.

"Then you ought to know better than I how he's doing."

I stammered something in reply.

"Does he show the proper diligence in the performance of his duties?" asked Melville, imitating the sniffy pomposity of collector Caruthers.

"His work is more than adequate," I replied blandly.

"He seemed a bright lad when I hired him."

"He has a good mind," I said.

"A good mind is hardly necessary here, as far as that goes. Still, it can't do any harm. If nothing else, he's someone you can talk to as you go about your business among the philistines. A good mind, you say? Perhaps I should avail myself of it. God knows, it's a rarity on the pier."

I smiled involuntarily at hearing my protégé praised, for so I was determined to think of him.

Melville studied his fingernails and then said, "You seem to take an interest in the boy."

His remark had been casually made, yet it troubled me. I shrugged without comment.

"Well, he's a likable young man," said Melville. "No harm in it."

The wind seemed to have gone out of our sails. Melville blew his nose energetically into a handkerchief large enough to rig a toy boat. I picked a loose thread from my cuff. He cleared his throat. We shifted in our chairs, creak answering creak. Our gazes roved about the room like flies unwilling to settle. A silence ensued that seemed an adjournment in a conversation waiting to be taken up again.

"How is Mrs. Melville?" I asked, hoping to change the subject.

"She's well."

"Please tell her I was asking for her."

"I'll do that, Shelby, and she'll no doubt be pleased by your interest," he replied with a particle of meanness in his expression.

"Tell her how much I enjoyed supper the other night."

I was fumbling—don't you see?—uncertain of myself and of how to proceed.

"I'll be sure to do that also."

He was looking intently at me.

"If there's any way I can be of—"

"Of what?"

He had brought me abruptly to a halt, from which I recovered with the grace of a lassoed steer.

"*Assistance!*" Having spoken too emphatically, I felt the guilt we sometimes do even though we're innocent. I tried again. "If I can ever do her a service, I'll do it gladly."

"Are you hoping to ingratiate yourself, Shelby? Do you find my wife so attractive that you'd court her under my very nose?"

I laughed nervously.

"Did I say something comical?" His gaze was scorching.

"I thought—"

"What did you think?"

"I must say, Herman, that your needling—"

Abruptly, he stood and took the harpoon in his hands.

"What?"

I was terrified, Roebling.

"You're hiding something."

"I—"

Before I could continue, he had heaved the harpoon at the wall opposite, where it bit deeply into the plaster.

I screamed, although the thing had not been aimed at me.

Melville laughed—you won't credit this, Roebling—he laughed good humoredly.

"I had you worried. Admit it: I had you heeling in the wind."

His moods, I knew by now, were variable. But this . . .

"It does a man good to be taken out of himself. Were you?"

"I was, yes; I was taken clear out of myself."

"Good!" he shouted, clapping me on the back. "We've arranged things too nicely, you and I and most other beneficiaries of the machine. We'll leave the poor aside, since they are the beneficiaries of naught, except what Christ promised them. We've smoothed the rough, ironed the rucks, graveled the dirt, and bricked over the gravel. We've glazed out the wind and cold and erased the sea's dragons painted on ancient maps and tamed its casual cruelties, so that Vanderbilt, Gould, and Morgan can enjoy pleasure cruises in steam yachts. Why, a man can put himself and his luggage on board a train at Grand Central Depot and, in less time than it took God to finish His universe, disembark at San Francisco! It's

unnatural, Shelby; it's not the life for which men were fashioned. We pretend we're higher than the animals and lower
than the angels, when all the time we're partly one and partly
the other. But mostly, we are beasts."

He went to the wall and pulled out the harpoon; it came
away with an effort. Plaster dust and horsehair clung to its
barbs. I would not have been surprised to see the wall bleed,
so deeply had the lance pierced it.

"I said that all we need to do is sit and wait for the world's
riches to come to us. There's the modern age in a nutshell.
We eat a pineapple or a coconut at Delmonico's and think we
have consumed the essence of Hawaii. We eat a plate of ver-
micelli and fancy ourselves Marco Polo. At tea, we're offered
a choice of "India" or "China," as though a handful of leaves
could stand for countries vast as continents! We fancy ourselves moguls, when, in actuality, we are scared little men."

Picking up a sheaf of papers on his desk, he rattled them
under my nose.

"Bills of lading, Shelby!" he exclaimed. "The spices of
Arabia, the wood Noah and his sons used to build the ark,
coffee 'cherries' grown in the forests of Ethiopia, on the foot-
hills of the Andes, plantations in Java, or the volcanic slopes
of Machu Picchu—the riches of the world are reduced to
barely legible scrawls on bills of lading. As if I could smell
the sea and feel it rolling beneath me while reading Richard
Henry Dana's book, or my own, for that matter."

In the grip of a powerful emotion, he was speaking to
someone not in the room.

"What is the whale oil we burn in our lamps or the

ambergris our ladies daub at their temples and throats next to the whale itself? What would they say if they knew that their spicy perfume began as dirty bile in the tripes of a whale? It vomits ambergris, which washes up onto the coasts of Africa, Madagascar, the Maldives, the Indies, the Molucca Islands, and Japan—unless a whaleman has already ripped open its belly and scooped out the aromatic stuff. What would the ladies say if they could see that raw lump of grease and smell the putrid carcass of the dead beast from whose bowels it was mined?"

Melville had become possessed by what, in contractual law, is called force majeure: an urging beyond human control, usually malevolent. He was pacing the narrow confines of our office as a captain does his bridge, alert to whales or warships, wind or maelstroms, Saint Elmo's fire or albatrosses.

"What is the story of a whale and its slaughter next to the animal itself and the hard and violent men who hunt it?" he asked, possibly of God, who might not have been listening. "Both commerce and literature squeeze essence from the thing itself—one for profit, the other for— What is it that makes us 'scorn delights and live laborious days'? God knows; I do not. It can't be fame or money." He laughed, as though a joke had been played on him, which, having long ago become inured to absurdity, he could appreciate. "They hunt symbols in my book, whereas Ahab hunted Moby Dick!"

I nearly asked him who Ahab was and what on earth was Moby Dick. (I had not then read the book.) But I was afraid to interrupt his oration, fueled by an increasing agitation. In such a voice, I imagined Daniel Webster delivered the eulogy for Major Melvill, Herman's zealot of a grandfather, as well as the infamous "Seventh of March Speech," which assured passage of the Missouri Compromise and prefigured Justice Taney and the Supreme Court's notorious decision in the case of *Dred Scott v. Sandford* confirming black people as chattel in law. Thus are linkages forged by which the world is moved and men enchained.

"There *was* an Ahab," said Melville, after having paused to drink some water. "His name was Captain John Fisher, a New Bedford man. In those days, most came from New Bedford—the captains and their crews and the whaling ships. The town was Quaker, and whaling one of the most necessary trades in the world at that time. Quaker frugality and universal necessity made New Bedford the richest place in Massachusetts. Its men went down to the sea in ships and, much too often, to the bottom with them. The last anyone saw of Fisher, he was tangled in ropes and clinging to the flank of a whale.

"Nowadays, men hunt whales for bones to stiffen ladies' corsets. How obscene that so colossal a creature should be annihilated to keep a woman trim! Do the ladies feel Leviathan underneath their dresses? Do they put on its knowledge with its power? Do they sense in their bones the nobility and prodigious force in its own? More than likely, they haven't an inkling of where their stays come from. An elephant, perhaps, or a buffalo—or a woolly mammoth."

Melville was spent of whatever emotion had driven him to fulminate against mankind, as Jonathan Edwards had done against the ungodly of New England. Millennia before him, Elijah had railed against Baal, and the Lord of Hosts against the Sodomites. In this world, there is no shortage of evildoers nor those who wish them otherwise. And should they prove intractable, there are plenty of good souls who will gladly help them into the next, if the villains don't cut their throats first.

I said nothing in response to his tirade. What was there for me to say?

Melville swept up the plaster dust his harpoon had caused.

"I gave you a fright, my friend," he said. "Fear can be as good for a man as a purge or a nose full of snuff."

I WENT TO THE SCALE HOUSE on Gansevoort Pier, where several customs men were engaged in weighing and measuring sacks of grain, raw sugar, and cocoa beans. Martin was laying iron weights in the pan of a scale. I watched as a sack slowly ascended until the balance beam was level with the floor. A shyness came over me, and I turned to leave, when he called to me.

"Hello, Mr. Ross."

"Mr. Finch," I nodded in reply.

We had addressed each other by our surnames, a formality seldom observed on the river, unless one of the customhouse trinity—the collector, naval officer, or surveyor—happened to be there. "Is everything as it should be?" The question was fatuous and impertinent, and the other men—Pintard, Cannon, Stephen Bowditch, Thomas

Foote, and the Hebrew Isaac Gutman—had raised their heads from their work and were regarding me curiously.

"Yes, sir."

"Good," I said gruffly as I left them to their tasks.

I was standing at the edge of the pier, watching an old-fashioned brig being warped into a slip, when Martin came up behind me.

"I wanted to apologize," he said hesitantly, "for having shirked last night. John Gibbs is the kind of bullying rough-neck I— I don't know how to deal with such men. I was humiliated. I'm useless in a fight. I'm very sorry, Shelby, for having let you down."

"I would no more have expected you to fight Gibbs than I would Ralph Waldo Emerson to take off his coat, roll up his sleeves, and put up his fists against a gin-stoked squarehead from the Bowery. I hit him because I've a temper, which often overrides common sense. What I can't fathom is why he didn't use his knife on me."

"And that ghastly moment when he put his arms around us . . ."

I could've sworn that Martin blushed, but maybe I was wrong.

"No, I can't fathom him at all. I'll tell you this, Martin: There was hatred in his eyes—they fairly glittered with it. Hatred and wickedness. Gibbs is a dangerous man, and you should be careful of him."

We stood and watched the river hurrying over the tidal strait from Long Island Sound to Upper New York Bay. So it has always done, and so, I suppose, will it ever do, in spite of us and our misdeeds. Martin spat into the water with a carelessness that made me shiver.

"I wanted to ask you about Melville."

"What about him?"

"The kind of novels that he writes."

My ignorance surprised Martin, who was bookish. "As far as I know, he writes only poetry now. But in the fifties, he rivaled Hawthorne as the greatest American writer of romances. I recall reading a review written long before I was born of *Moby-Dick* that asked, 'Who knows the terrors of the sea like Herman Melville?'"

"Who or what is Moby Dick?"

"A great white whale, which bit off Captain Ahab's leg and left him with an everlasting rage. It's a stupendous book!"

"I've never heard of it."

"Well, it did sink into the graveyard of forgotten novels. I suppose there's not a man on this pier, except Melville and myself, who's read it. When he hired me, I shook his hand and told him how much the book had meant to me. He thanked me brusquely and said that his past was his own affair. He appeared to be embarrassed by it."

"I'd like to read it."

"I had a first edition, but sadly, I left it behind in Argentina. I gave it to a friend."

That Martin Finch should have lived, however briefly, in South America amazed me. In his physique and temperament, he seemed unsuited to an adventure abroad.

"I'd never have believed you were the sort to rough it."

Three years before, Martin and his brother, Franklin,

had gone to Buenos Aires to establish an import business at a time when the gold peso was strong and the Argentinian economy thriving. They'd failed because of ineptitude, while American merchants who had managed things better prospered. Here are two more bankrupts for the club, I told myself.

"It took us a year to realize we'd never make a go of it. I came home with nothing to show for my time and effort, except malaria. Franklin took up his trade again, and I, who had none, cast about for a time until I was taken on at the pier."

"You must have brought back a few stories of your own."

"I suppose," he replied thoughtfully. "But you needn't go all the way to Buenos Aires to have an adventure. You've only to walk down to the Battery."

He had spoken like a conspirator—or so it seemed to me—and I chose not to take his meaning, if indeed he had meant anything by his remark.

"Melville said we have only to wait, and the world will come to us."

"If you want to read *Moby-Dick*, the Mercantile Library is sure to own a copy."

"Where would that be?"

"Lafayette Street, near Astor Place. If you want, we can go there together."

I agreed, and in his excitement, he told me the story of Ishmael on board the *Pequod*.

The Mercantile Library at East Eighth Street, Lafayette Street, and Astor Place, April 17, 1882

Having finished our work for the day, Martin and I walked toward Lafayette Street, stopping in Greenwich Lane to appease our hunger at a Jews' eating house with pickled herring, bread, and a soup made of rendered chicken fat. Shortly afterward, we were mounting the granite steps of the Mercantile Library. The pamphlet describes it in glorious terms. I'll read you the preamble:

> Designed by Isaiah Rogers in the Greek Revivalist style espoused by Thomas Jefferson, the building known today as the Mercantile Library of New York features classical arcades, columns and pilasters in the Doric mode, chaste entablatures, and imposing gables characteristic of our nation's grand civic architecture. In its frank and forthright manner and its lofty dignity, this architectural ideal is the perfect expression in wood and stone of our democracy. The building was commissioned by the Astor Place Opera, whose first performance, on November 22, 1847, was Giuseppe Verdi's *Ernani*.

You may have the pamphlet to kindle your stove.

As an opera house, the building would have been

imposing—perhaps too much so for an expression of democracy in wood and stone, which no poor man or woman could enter unless it was to clean the marble floors. And what could Ernani have meant to Michael Flagherty of shantytown, although, if he'd known Ernani had been a bandit, he might have been curious to hear his story shrieked and bellowed from the stage. The city's down-and-out have far less exclusive places in which to hear the songs of laundresses, their voices coarsened by steam, and the comic patter of porters and road menders.

The pamphlet also summarizes the Astor Place Riot, of May 1849, when the opera house became known as the "Massacre Opera House at Dis-Astor Place." In 1854, the building was resurrected as the Mercantile Library. Like a resourceful storyteller, history knits an endless yarn.

Do you know the story of the riot? It's delicious in its way, and who knows, but there might be some truth in it?

A mob of Irish immigrants and lawless Bowery Boys gutted the opera house during a performance of *Macbeth*. Had they gotten their hands on him, they'd have filleted William Macready, the English actor playing the Scottish usurper, as well as the English-loving ladies and gents in their evening clothes. The rioters marched up Broadway, breaking windows with brickbats and paving stones and looting the palaces of the nouveau riche. The reason for the mayhem was the common people's hatred of all things British, incorporated in Macready. The people's man, the American Edwin Forrest, who'd begun his career on the makeshift stages of the Lower East Side, happened to be playing Macbeth at the Broadway Theatre. The rabble would have crowned him king of New York had the coup de théâtre succeeded, but the infantry and hussars of the Seventh Regiment put down the bloody riot most bloodily. With the help of John Jacob Astor and Washington Irving, Macready escaped harm. According to the pamphlet, New York City policemen would henceforth walk their beats armed.

Have you been inside the library? There's a landscape by Frederic Church. As a young man, he went on voyages in search of subject matter. The same could be said of Melville. In *El Río de Luz*, Church recalled in oil paint what his eyes had seen in South America in 1857. The painting is three times removed from the scene it depicts, which may be the Amazon or else a composite of lesser rivers. First, there is the river itself, then Church's memory of it altered by twenty years of recollection, and finally the painting in the Mercantile Library.

Your bridge will be diminished by photographs and stereopticon cards, postcards and engravings, paintings and poems. With each new rendering, it will grow smaller, until one day it will be no more than a symbol and a souvenir. I've seen the Great Pyramid at Giza reproduced in colored inks in an advertisement for a burial fund society. Even pharaohs become as common as dust.

Am I being overly philosophic? Well, success has nothing to teach; it's our failures that turn us into philosophers, or liars. And I have had my share of failure. Forgive my pedantry and self-pity; they are unattractive qualities.

The library's collection runs to two hundred thousand

books—an order of magnitude appropriate to astronomy or to the fourteen thousand miles of steel wire holding up your bridge. I felt insignificant, walking through its marbled rooms to the sound of my footsteps echoing in the vaulted ceiling. Pedestrians will feel the same humbling as they walk high above the East River, like aerialists in Barnum's circus—at a penny a crossing.

Martin and I were pacing an aisle that began with Defoe's *Journal of the Plague Year* and ended with Erasmus's *Praise of Folly*.

"I come here frequently. I feel . . ."

"What do you feel, Martin?"

"It might sound foolish, but I feel safe and nourished."

Like a rat in a granary, I thought at the time.

"As if I were standing behind heavy iron doors locked from the inside."

Like those at the Harper's Ferry engine house, before the marines battered them down and took John Brown captive.

"Here we are," he said as we came athwart the shelf where Herman Melville's books lay.

"So many!" I exclaimed, running a finger across the spines. "I'd never have guessed that he had written so many. Nor that there would be so much dust," I said, showing Martin my gray-felted finger.

"He's gone out of fashion. Here's the book you want: *Moby-Dick; or, The Whale*." He hauled out a thick volume published in 1851 by Harper & Brothers, New York, bound in green cloth.

"I wish he'd been briefer. There must be enough wind inside to fill a mainsail."

"Not a word but what is necessary," said Martin with slight umbrage, I thought. "He wasn't writing a bill of lading."

"I'll borrow it and tell you what I think."

"I've been wanting to read *Redburn* again," said Martin, taking down the first of that novel's two volumes. "Melville created a character named Harry Bolton, whom I've not been able to forget."

Weighing *Moby-Dick* in my hand, I wondered how long it would take to get through it.

"Redburn, an American sailor, takes a guide book that belonged to his father on a voyage to Liverpool, wanting to retrace his dead sire's footsteps," explained Martin. "But the book was sadly out-of-date, and the ghost of Redburn's father nowhere to be found." Martin glanced at me. "There's a meaning there," he said, with a rising inflection, like a teacher prodding a lazy pupil. "An unpleasant truth."

I gave him a flippant reply. "Stories seldom have much to do with the real world, and they come as close to the truth of their subject as Griffith's *Street Directory of Brooklyn* does to Brooklyn."

Martin regarded me skeptically. "If we weren't shut up in our own petty selves, there would be no need for other people's stories." He'd spoken like someone minting an epigram. Well, I've launched more than a few of my own. Vanity—by the pinch or the pound—is mixed into the dough and leaven of us all.

He tucked *Redburn* under his arm and started toward

the clerk who would note its loan to him as well as that of *Moby-Dick* to me. At a reading table, beneath a green-shaded lamp, an old man wearing sleeve protectors had fallen asleep over a portfolio of antique maps, his old-fashioned Burnside whiskers crushed against the Iberian Peninsula during the reign of Augustus.

The door leading to the street seemed heavier than it had, as though its wood and brass had been replaced by stone.

NIGHT HAD FALLEN ON THE FINE HOUSES of the rich in Astor Place and Broadway and on the hovels of the Five Points, though we were not near the latter to verify the fact. "Facts," Melville had said, "are verifiable by the scale and by the measuring stick, but what the heart desires and what thoughts the mind entertains can only be conjectured." "I'd have thought that was obvious," I replied, a remark that left him scowling at his paperwork. I know now—and have already said as much—that sometimes the obvious hides truths that can be as profound as those we hunt for in obscurity.

The night being mild, Martin and I walked up Broadway to Bowery Road, where George Washington sits astride his bronze horse in Union Square. We agreed that John Gibbs was vile and possibly insane.

"Do you think he means us harm?" asked Martin carefully.

"He's a mean dog on a short chain," I said. "So long as we keep out of his way, we've nothing to fear." I hoped I had sounded convincing. I was not convinced.

"I'd feel better if he were to disappear."

Grant would have thought the same about Lee before the Battle of Appomattox Courthouse.

A newsboy swaggered down the brick pavement as brazenly as a Tammany Hall thug. He shouted the evening headlines the way another boy would hawk his apples. "'Treacherous Outbreak by Apaches!' ... 'Incredible Tales of Ruin in Brownsville!' ... 'Brilliant Auroral Display in Poughkeepsie!' ... 'Serious Interference with Telegraphic Communication!'"

The boy could have arrived from the world of Tom Sawyer and Huckleberry Finn, except that his teeth were rotted, a cigarette was pasted to his lower lip, and I'd likely find a jackknife in his pocket used for games more serious than mumblety-peg.

"Paper, gents?" he asked, combing back his soap locks with his fingers.

"No thank you," I said.

"Ah, come on! Don't be that way! Give us a penny, and I'll give you the *World*."

I gave him a penny to be rid of him.

I gave Martin the front page; I took the shipping news. We perused them under the gaslights, our inward visions lively with savages and sailing departures, respectively. For all we were aware of our surroundings, Washington could have gotten down from his high horse and gone to supper at Fraunces Tavern, where a century before, he'd bidden farewell to the officers of the Continental Army. The park had dissolved into newsprint, and words had taken the place of reality. If a penny newspaper could materialize bloodthirsty

Apaches and a cyclone in Union Square, what effect could Melville's novel have on an impressionable mind? To one like Martin's, the *Pequod* could appear among the departures from the Port of New York. But I had no such mind and saw only printed columns devoted to tonnage.

What did appear before our eyes was a prostitute; by her dress and demeanor, she could have been nothing else. She sidled like a cat, only not so winsomely. She was much the worse for drink, as my father often said of his brother, Thomas, who fell during the Great Skedaddle. I've always hoped that he was the worse for drink at the moment of his death and exhaled his boozy breath into the face of Saint Peter, who when he'd been only Simon the fisherman liked his tipple. Sobriety is a great virtue in maiden aunts, Methodist deacons, and the like, who do not go to sea or war.

"She's as common as a barber's chair that a troop of cavalry has mounted," I said to Martin, recalling a colorful figure of speech heard on the docks, if not found anywhere in the New York Mercantile Library. At that moment, I wanted to sound coarse and insensitive, like a common tough.

Martin laughed, perhaps for the same reason.

And then, Roebling, as abruptly as the woman had stepped into the ring of gaslight cast onto the walk, I felt in some duct or organ a red-hot shame. I had on my lips words such as "She is to be pitied," but I never spoke them. I can think of no other nation whose citizens do not think of it as their fatherland or motherland. Americans are fatherless and motherless and—because of it—pitiless.

We're orphans. Left on our own to make our way, we are a country of tricksters and hard scrabblers.

The night no longer seemed kind. Both Martin and I fell into a "brown study," an expression lovelier than what it means.

I stood and wished Martin a good night. Walking home to my room, I couldn't get out of my own shadow. "A shadow is a metaphor for the invisible and ineffable," Melville had once said. "And a metaphor is the shadow of a truth. Those who behold it are struck blind or driven insane." Was he talking about himself or Ahab?

West Street Customs Office, April 19, 1882

While I waited for Melville to arrive and assign me a cargo to appraise, I continued the reading I'd begun two nights before in *Moby-Dick*. I had reached the chapter in which Father Mapple delivers his sermon to the sailors at the New Bedford Whaleman's Chapel. I remember these lines in particular:

> . . . in all this raging tumult, Jonah sleeps
> his hideous sleep. He sees no black sky and
> raging sea, feels not the reeling timbers, and
> little hears he or heeds he the far rush of the
> mighty whale, which even now with open
> mouth is cleaving the seas after him.

My interest in Melville's novel was not so great that I resented the time when I could not read more of it; neither was it so slight that I was eager to close the book and return it to the Mercantile Library, although I confess to having skipped the "Extracts (Supplied by a Sub-sub-Librarian)." My head was buried in the book, but it was not, as in the case of dull, soporific works, such as collected homilies or histories of the thirteen colonies, pillowed on it. I was picturing myself in New Bedford, sitting in a pew next to Queequeg, the tattooed cannibal, when Melville entered the room. He saw his book and was not pleased.

"An author is no more grateful to a reader of his failures than a formerly pretty woman to her mirror for reminding her of the pox that left her scarred."

"I'm enjoying it, Herman." I stretched the truth as anyone would to a superior.

"Then you are in a minority, or what writers like to call an 'elite readership.' In the thirty years since *Moby-Dick* first appeared in America and Great Britain, it has sold fewer than four thousand copies. I don't expect that Death, whenever he chooses to show himself, will burnish my dulled reputation, but for Lizzie's sake, I hope I'm wrong. Now kindly put the book away. In any case, the problems of the universe are humbug."

With a petulant and resounding thud, I closed it on the page in which Queequeg signs aboard the *Pequod*. Sublimely indifferent to the glories of our civilization—as if to read and write were well beside the point of existence—the cannibal harpooner makes his mark, identical to one tattooed on his arm:

Quohog.
His ✠ mark.

"If you're excited by exotica, read this," said Melville, handing me a customs declaration. "A consignment of sugarcane from Suriname awaits your pleasure aboard the *Panama*. I would like it cleared by six o'clock. The Griswolds want to collect it in the morning."

I told him it would be done on time, knowing that in all probability it wouldn't. The slumgullions of the Customs Service are Whitman's ideal democratic type: They "lean and loaf at [their] ease observing a spear of summer grass." To be honest, they are more likely to observe their gobs of spit, as though their future could be scried in them.

As I was leaving, Melville said, "Your friend Finch had an accident yesterday."

"When?"

"Near to quitting time."

I was unaware of it, having been at the New York Custom House to get the surveyor's signature on a number of documents of title. One of the perquisites of my job in the so-called "outside force" is an occasional visit to Wall Street to "confer" with my superiors, who are legion and barely sensible of my existence. I'm uncomfortable there. I seem always to be made to feel a transient whose genteel shabbiness is conspicuous among those at home in the marbled halls of power. My linen feels unclean. To their refined sense of smell, my clothes must reek of fish and tar.

"What happened?" I let my voice go where it will.

"A pallet loaded with barrels of Indian meal fell on him." He saw my dismay and hurried to assure me that Martin wasn't dead. "At the last moment, he stepped aside, or he'd be lying stiff on a pair of trestles."

"How could such a thing happen?" I said with the casual curiosity that a stray dog run down in the street would arouse. The docks are no place to be maudlin.

"The break on the steam donkey let go, and Martin's foot was badly injured."

Not so bad as your father's, Roebling, crushed by a Fulton Ferry steamer.

"He's had the doctor to see him and should return to work in three or four weeks, barring complications."

Complications—the grit in the gear that frustrates our calculations!

Melville had paused and would presently spoon out the rest of the medicine for me to swallow. "He lost two toes."

I wondered idly how many toes a person could lose and still walk unaided.

"I've known men who've lost more than their toes," said Melville brusquely.

I laughed as one sometimes will at a particularly vicious or offensive joke. How often do we try to make ourselves out to be brutes?

"John Gibbs will be your weigher on the *Panama*."

Melville looked at me carefully, knowing, I suppose, how much I hated Gibbs.

Chance exerts its own influence over the affairs of men. It had brought me into a fateful conjunction with John

Gibbs, and with his opposite in temperament, Martin Finch. Had there never been a panic and depression, I could have escaped my end—or more likely not. The wind that blows ill would have found me, bear away though I might. There are cannibals abroad on the island of Manhattan, who never get closer to the South Seas than whale oil and ambergris. They lie in ambush, waiting for us to make our inevitable mistakes.

I climbed down into the hold of the *Panama* as one would descend into a pit of vipers. The hairs on the back of my neck stood up while my heart beat to an accompaniment of an odd whistling in my nose. In short, I was afraid. Encountering Gibbs sitting on a barrel, however, I was surprised to hear him greet me pleasantly, as if I'd never drawn a knife on him or bloodied his lip and nose.

"Hello, Mr. Ross," he said in his oiliest tone. "Keeping well, I hope?"

"I am, thank you. And you?"

"Tolerably."

We went on in this genteel way like two acquaintances meeting by chance at the bourse.

"I'm sorry we got off on the wrong foot," he said. (Had he used the word *foot* deliberately to make me think of Martin's accident?)

"I should not have gone for you. I lost my temper. I never wished anyone harm before."

A lie, of course. I had prayed often that a painful end would befall my creditors and especially Jay Gould and "Diamond Jim" Fisk, who happily would be shot dead in the Grand Central Hotel by Edward Stokes, another bankrupt. I'd be delighted if the whole gang of robber barons, crooks, and cutthroat moneymen of the Gilded Age would be torn limb from limb by a god of any persuasion, not excluding pagan, so long as he or she or it were inhumanly cruel and vengeful.

"What do you say we speak no more of it?" asked a conciliatory Gibbs.

At that moment, he looked like a perfectly ordinary man, if not a gentleman. You could encounter his like in the park or at the Battery, feeding pigeons. He might have been a genial cabman or a good-natured grocer filling a luckless widow's reticule with turnips at a penny the pound.

"Agreed?" he asked, extending a hand, which I took. Relieved and grateful, I could have kissed it.

We set to work and soon were in fine spirits. I had believed myself to be an excellent judge of character but was happy to have misjudged Gibbs. It would not have done any good to have persisted in our hostility. Our occupation brought us together in dusky holds, in the gloomy scale house, and on the sometimes desolate pier. It would be easy to rip a man with the hook or knife or tip him into the river. My body could have caught the outbound tide and ended in the Atlantic. While it's true I'd often wished harm upon my fellow men, I had neither the physique nor the sanguinary instinct necessary to kill one of them. I had a short fuse but lacked the lethal charge required to lay waste to my enemies.

And what *had* Gibbs done to me? Ridiculed my clothes. Melville had done the same on my first morning in his office. I'd looked ridiculous and was deserving of their scorn. Gibbs had dirtied my boot with a stream of tobacco juice, but I'd been wearing rubber boots. No harm was done. I was the one who had picked up the knife and lunged at him. And Sunday? He'd breathed booze into my face, for which he'd been sorry.

Having finished our work, Gibbs spiled a cask of Holland gin and filled a bucket with it before pegging the barrel closed. Snobs profess an aversion to gin, looking down their noses or pinching their nostrils in supercilious disgust. But like my father before me, I've always relished the drink for its clarity and the fragrance of juniper berries. Like Charles Dickens's Mr. Jarndyce or Sarah Gamp, who lived on cucumbers and gin, I'd be content to sit by the fire on a nippy night and sip "Dutch water" till Morpheus descended or the cows came home.

Gibbs ladled out gin from the bucket, drank it, and, having drawn another ladleful, gave it to me.

I hesitated.

"What's wrong?" he asked with what might have been a momentary cunning in his eyes. "Whatever was in that old bilge barrel died a happy death in good Dutch gin," he said. "Or is it that I took the first drink? Are you too refined to put your lips where mine have been?"

I shivered, as if ice had formed in the hollows of my bones, though the day was mild and I stood within a beam of sunshine, which reached down into the hold.

"Never fear!" said Gibbs, laughing merrily. "I don't have 'bad blood' or the 'Spanish disease.'" He gave me a peculiar look and said, "I'm free of what can come of lying with a woman."

Something shaped itself in my mind—a nameless, featureless disquiet—but I shook it off and in a moment had downed the ladle's worth of gin. Instantly, I felt the good of it.

"There's a good lad!" shouted Gibbs. To be called a "lad" at my age—I was nearly forty—struck me as comical, and I laughed because of the gin, I suppose, which was already giddying my brain.

Gibbs?

I'd say he has ten years on me. He is grayish, unhealthy-looking—his hair and face, both gray. He looks like someone who has spent his years in the boiler rooms of ships and in the barrooms of ports. I've seen many men who look so. I wonder if your Irish sandhogs do after their years down inside the caissons. "The fetid stables of nightmares" Melville called them.

Gibbs drank another ladleful, and at his encouragement, which seemed, now that I recall it, to have centered in his eyes, I followed his example.

We sat on some fardage. He sang a sailor's ditty, salty as a kippered herring. I can't recall the words; I remember thinking it was funny. He chucked me on the chin and called me a "grand fellow." I leaned my head against a barrel—by now I was drunk—and he spoke in a low voice. I could feel his moist breath against my ear. My eyes closed as though draper's weights were fastened to the lids. I felt the ship roll under me, though it might have been only my gut that heaved. I was sick on the floor. Gibbs gave me more gin to wash out my sour mouth. I laid down on burlap ticking and felt his hand crawling on me, loathsome as a rat. I swatted it away, spat out my disgust as you would rancid meat, and before I fell into the waters of oblivion, I called him a vile name. The word escapes me. He stood and gave me a savage kick, and that was all I knew.

Two years have passed since Ross related
the first part of his story.
The Brooklyn Bridge is now finished.

On May 17, 1884, P. T. Barnum leads
a troupe of elephants across it.
On this day, Ross narrates
the end of his story.

Part Two

Barnum & the Elephants

Washington Roebling's Second-Story Room on Brooklyn Heights, May 17, 1884

Two years have passed since we were together in this room. You finished your work and went home to Trenton. I finished mine and went to prison. Much has happened, but I dare say we are much the same as before. The rise and fall—of a man or an empire—takes time to accomplish. Rome wasn't built—nor did it end—in a day. I expect to go on awhile longer.

Melville? He goes on as always. He's the rock on which he dashes himself to pieces.

In my cell, I read his adventure stories, *Typee*, *Omoo*, *White-Jacket*, and *Moby-Dick*. I'll read them again on lonely, damp winter nights with the coal stove roaring like Ahab's own ocean or curses. I'm no Ahab, Roebling, except in the immensity of the hatred I conceived for John Gibbs. It had been simmering for months, but the boiling over seems to have taken hardly any time at all. Three weeks ... four. When it did rise up in me, it was scalding.

Ahab. A man with such a name could never be a cringer, a worrier after his virtue and his purse, a petitioner whose whimper has turned hoarse in supplication, whose trouser knees are worn, whose head is bowed and back is bent, whose element is a slurry of cinders, wet ash, and horses' stale staining the winter snow through which he tramps resignedly from almshouse to poorhouse until he is carried to his last and smallest house, a plain coffin in a pauper's grave. Not that I'm any of those things, mind you; I never once begged the judge for mercy. But my fury did not last, and, like a pot taken off the boil, the hatred subsided when the cause was removed.

What a name is Ahab! To be called thus must sever a boy from dependency, put iron in his marrow, and make a cold forge of the heart. It is a name to blow him out of childhood into the fullness of life, never mind the cost. Only a man of uncommon strength of will can bear the name of the seventh king of Israel and the ruler of Moab, whose corpse was defiled by dogs and swine, according to the prophecy of Isaiah, and whom God hated.

I shouldn't mind being hated by Him if I could be in the company of such a man, even if he was laid waste in Gilead and buried in a sty. King Ahab roared his defiance, as I would wish to do mine when the time comes. Melville's famous captain did the same, although I'd sooner have been in the retinue of the Israelite than aboard the *Pequod* with its crazed master and crew. Ahab—raised in the Holy Land or in Nantucket—was accursed by God. Sometimes I think I am, as well, although my Christian name would suit an effete poet or a parlor snake.

We all come at last to our story's end, and I don't give a damn if my husk, after the great winnowing, molders in the ground on Ward's Island or in my father's crypt at Green-Wood Cemetery—a pleasure park for cast-off flesh soon to be no more. Our bones are none the worse for common dirt, so long as they danced when the body was quick. That was the philosophy of my father, who began life a poor boy and ended it in the handsome tomb of a merchant prince. Having been rich for a time, he'd had the foresight to buy a vault in which he and his heirs could dwell "in perpetuity"—a condition existing nowhere except in the deed to a cemetery allotment.

In prison, I had two years to ponder the Wheel of Fortune's having turned against me. In my fancy, I chose to think of them as a sojourn on one of the Heliades, the seven islands in the Ocean Stream, where the people of the sun still live amid grape and fig vines, pear and apple trees. Some good came of my classical education after all! In my story, I owed my escape to Melville, who rowed me across the harbor to a waiting ship, just as the grown Pip had done for Magwitch. He was taken and drowned, but in my day-dreams I fared better. I embarked on the *Highlander*, captained by a saintly man, which carried me, as in a dream, to the ocean between India and Ethiopia, called the Arabian Sea. I know why we tell one another stories. The reason is not, as Martin claimed, to console us for having only one life to call our own; stories help us to endure it.

You're a good listener, Roebling, if a laconic one. Your confinement makes you hungry for tales having nothing to do with metallurgy, mathematics, and catenary curves. And what in hell *is* a catenary curve? Never mind—I'm certain not to understand it. But what a magnificent thing your mind has wrought, my friend! And we both have lived to see it.

I'm glad you let me visit you again. I was afraid you'd shun me. We're much alike, I think. We are *Isolatos*—you, by reason of your sickness, and I, well, because I'm a bankrupt whose tastes are too elevated for his purse, which is too meager for the requirements of polite society. The patricians disdain my penury far more than the fact of my imprisonment. Why, some of the wealthiest men have been crooks: Boss Tweed, Thomas Durant, the rascal behind the Crédit Mobilier scandal and the Union Pacific "con," Gould and Frick—and your contractor J. Lloyd Haigh, who is now breaking rocks at Sing Sing for having sold you inferior wire for the cables. The whole shebang could have fallen down like "London Bridge" had the fraud not come to light! Crooks, one and all, and yet they were accounted men of eminence and rank.

I called Durant a "rascal." The words we use for villainy are, like *villain* itself, ridiculous to modern ears. *Reprobate. Scoundrel. Ruffian. Roughneck. Rogue.* I might just as well have called him a "whoreson dog" or a "jacksauce," as in Shakespeare's day—or a memorable phrase by Alexander

Pope, which Melville used when he disparaged Collector of Customs Caruthers as a "mere white curd of Ass's milk!" The wickedness of this century has outrun our vocabulary, and I suppose it will be left to the future to say what we truly were in our time. What will *evil* mean, I wonder, in the twentieth century? What range, resources, and ruthlessness will it imply?

In this city, which the world calls "great," there are those who will not be swayed by sentiment or suffer their purposes to be altered, who recoil at human frailty, and chafe at the restraints imposed by lawmakers and churchmen. They would give the Devil title to their soul and sign all requisite conveyances in their own blood before they'd see their schemes come to naught. They won't blandish or fawn—no, not even at Doomsday, when, dressed in silken shrouds, they demand to be let in through heaven's gate. I once fancied myself one of them. I might have been one still had circumstances not humbled me—had not ironed me flat. If only there were a drawing salve we could smear on our breast and be rid of all the poisons that waste us, body and soul! I wish He had made me other than I was.

I recall reading in the *Herald* the early stories on the bends, which struck the diggers inside the second caisson. Caisson sickness nearly finished you. Having escaped burning and drowning, you became disabled by the very air you breathed inside that ghastly tomb. Your invalidism could have spelled disaster for the project—in the tabloids at any rate, those stew pots of hearsay and scandal. But the bridge stands, complete and miraculous, and has only to await Barnum's stunt to allay the public's fear that it will collapse. If only we could do the same for the airy structures our minds create out of nothing but desire and on which we raise our lives as though on bedrock! How reassuring it would be if Barnum's elephants could march across our schemes and prove their worthiness, if only to ourselves!

Yes, I read it in the papers at the time: The Manhattan tower rests on sand. You stopped thirty feet short of bedrock, knowing the bridge would be upheld by mathematics. It was a gamble, and one we all must take eventually: to hazard "our Lives, our Fortunes and our sacred Honor" on an uncertain foundation. Barnum is for Barnum, and it's a silly business to rely on pachyderms for proof! But they will prove you correct, Roebling, once they've plodded across the river from Manhattan to Brooklyn. Your bridge will still be standing.

If you like, I'll finish the story I began two years ago. I'll tell you how my life slipped out from under me.

The Slide at 157 Bleecker Street, the Bowery, April 24, 1882

I didn't visit Martin for a week after the accident. There was no reason I should have gone sooner. What purpose would have been served? We were not bound like the Siamese twins Chang and Eng, whom I once saw at Barnum's circus. Would you call them twins, or being indivisible, did they constitute a single person? In any case, Martin and I were no more than friends, and only once have I felt the attachment for another that surpasses all the rest.

In his absence, Gibbs and I worked together, and as he'd

done previously, he acted as if nothing extraordinary had passed between us. He was downright amiable and behaved toward me in a manner he must have thought charming. He was all smiles and pleasantries and would bring me small treats to savor: a jar of oysters, a slab of gammon, a cold meat pie, and once a sea cucumber from the chink's doggery on Mott Street, which I couldn't stomach. Each night when we parted, he'd pat my shoulder and wish me a safe journey home. He appeared to be a changed man, but I never trusted him. I don't believe in the reformation of churches or of men. God and His creatures are immutable, or else the world would unravel into nothing, like a ball of wool.

I recall one afternoon in particular: We had gone down into the hold of a Dutch merchant ship to weigh and appraise a shipment of woolen cloth from Leyden.

"How is friend Martin?" asked Gibbs solicitously. "I hope his foot is mending."

We had paused to smoke a cigar.

"Why should I know or care what's become of Martin Finch?" I replied waspishly. It was a foolish question—the reflex action, say, of a starfish, one of whose arms has been poked with a stick.

"Why, isn't he your friend?" asked Gibbs, amazed. "Before the poor fellow's accident, you two were thick as thieves."

"We are acquaintances."

He sniffed and his nostrils flared. Had he been a bloodhound, he'd have bayed at the scent of a discovery worth the hunt and worthy of being torn apart.

"We have interests in common."

"Ah! Reading books and such."

Had he followed us to the library?

"We enjoy a yarn," I said with the air of a man who likes to sit around a barrel of corn whiskey and guffaw over a vicious tale with his fellow good-for-nothings.

"We all do!" said Gibbs, and laughed. "A good yarn beats diddling a woman's cunny. Am I right, Shelby?"

I could feel my face redden. "I don't know about that!" I said, accompanied by what I judged to be an indecent wink.

"Ha! There's the lad!" He smoked his cigar thoughtfully and then said, "Let's you and me go see what the world of men is really like."

He noted my hesitation.

"Come on, man! I'll show you the sights of the city you missed when you were a big bug uptown. Unless you'd rather visit an injured friend," he simpered tenderly. "Were you planning to see poor Martin Finch tonight?"

"No," I snapped. "Why would I be?"

"Then you'll let me take you on a trip to the Bowery, the pesthole where I grew up."

I agreed. What else could I have done?

WE RODE A HORSECAR DOWN HUDSON STREET to Bleecker and then walked to a disreputable-looking house at number 157. It was like any other house in the street, save that through its windows I could see men and women behaving as though the curtains were not open to the inspection of the curious.

"Welcome to the Slide, Shelby!" said Gibbs, rubbing his hands together in anticipation. Had they been wooden instead of flesh, they'd have burst into flame. "Though we frequenters of the place call it 'the Palace of Aladdin,' in view of its manifold delights."

We went inside the vestibule and, pushing through a beaded curtain, stepped into a large room infernally illuminated by gas fixtures, where every manner of vice was on display. I won't bore you with a catalogue, Roebling, which would be varied and sordid. Suffice it to say, I'd never before encountered such depraved goings-on, except in the pages of *The Pearl*, which I threw into the fire in disgust.

A particularly wicked image is engraved on my memory: A woman was kneeling before a rowdy, who looked never to have bathed. Roebling, you are a man of the world and know that sometimes we will stumble on a forbidden scene and cannot tear our eyes away. I'm ashamed to have stood there openmouthed and watched as all around me men and women were behaving with equal shamelessness. But the worst was yet to come. Gibbs went to the kneeling woman, whispered in her ear something that made her smile, and then pulled quickly at her hair, which came away in his hands! It was then I realized that the woman was a man!

The viperous congregation turned to me while, one by one, the women changed their gender as easily as you doff your hat. They regarded me with amusement, their faces sweaty and evil-looking, paint and rouge smeared, their wigs clutched in hands whose fingernails were long and lacquered. I could have vomited on the Turkish rug, where damascene pillows suggested to my overheated fancy the languid attitudes of vice. I was overcome by nausea. I pinched my arm like a child, hoping to find that I was dreaming. Roebling, I did not know where to set my eyes! So this is Whitman's "manly attachments" and "athletic love!" I said to myself, feeling revulsion for the old man. Then they came at me, slithering on all fours like snakes. I was sinking into the delirium experienced by drunkards at the frothy frontier of madness.

You may think that I made too much of it, Roebling; that I had only to turn on my heels to put the scene behind me. But I was gripped by a debility—what you and the sandhogs would have felt when oppressed by the malady of men out of their depth. Had the house—a house such as Edgar Poe would have lovingly described—been set afire by the torches of an outraged mob gathered in the street, I could not have moved—no, not even to save myself from burning.

I stood, immobile and oddly impassive, while the savages pulled me to the floor and ate me—faces turned to masks of greedy appetite, and their hands and mouths turned bloodred by the ruby-shaded lamps.

I don't know why I'm telling you this story, of all the stories that constitute my life. It feels as though it never happened, or happened to somebody else. Even now I look back on that night in disbelief, like a man who caught his reflection doing something shameful in a mirror. That's the way of stories, and why we're right to fear them.

While I lay upon the floor, my mind passed in and out of darkness like a leaf moving in a breeze from light into shade and back again. At times, the room was black as pitch; at others, it was lighted by the lamps' lurid shades. Awakened, I longed for darkness and insensibility, but no sooner had I lapsed into stupefaction than I would be roughly brought to consciousness by a jarring noise or rude handling and would feel, upon emerging from my "caisson," a gnawing on my bones.

Was I imagining it?

I don't know; I might have been. I was beside myself. A nice expression—don't you think? It draws a picture of me standing next to some other me. A Chang and Eng! I saw, or thought I did, the hideous Gibbs. He seemed to be everywhere in the room—more goatish satyr than a man. He was the image and definition of depravity. The worst of it was, I knew that I'd struck a bargain with him, whose terms had yet to be disclosed.

The Finches' House in Maiden Lane, April 25, 1882

The following day, I sent word to Melville that I'd taken sick. I did not say that the trouble lay within my soul. Maybe I should have; few others could have understood that organ and its maladies better than he. I wanted to be by myself awhile and worry the sharp tooth of guilt. I had done nothing worse at the Slide than to succumb to inertia. What others may have done to me cannot be charged to my account by an earthly or a heavenly tribunal. But conscience can be perverse, assigning guilt where none is deserved.

I wanted to atone!

I say again, Roebling, that I had nothing *for* which to

atone. In any case, I felt guilty that I had not yet paid Martin a visit. He'd been charming company, and we'd grown close enough in spirit to speak frankly in a world where candor is seldom possible and rarely welcomed. Damn it, I had valued Martin as a friend and saw no reason why I shouldn't visit him!

I rode an omnibus down Eighth as far as Greenwich Lane, then walked east to Broadway. The marvelous air and light and many scenes of contentment along the great thoroughfare were tonic for one whose mind was in turmoil. The locusts were already blooming, and the chestnuts seemed impatient to show their blossoms. On such a day, the world rediscovers its instinctual leaning toward spring and clemency. I studied the shop windows, thinking that I ought to buy a gift for Martin after having neglected him. In a bookseller's on Broome Street, I hunted among volumes of poetry for one whose gift would not be misconstrued. Tennyson, perhaps, or Keats. And then my eyes lighted on a book by Melville: *Clarel: A Poem and Pilgrimage in the Holy Land.* I bought it at once, persuaded by its subtitle, although I was ignorant of its contents.

In Canal Street, I bought three cigars—for Martin, Franklin, and me. There are few places as pleasant as a tobacconist's. One can stand and dream amid the humidors of the fragrant ends of the earth.

Arriving at the Finches' house in Maiden Lane, I knocked and was shown inside by Franklin's wife, whom I hadn't met during my first visit. She's a pretty woman, no older, I would guess, than thirty. She has an Irish colleen's face, fair and lightly freckled; her eyes are green and flecked with gold; her smile is warm, her hair russet. She'd been in the kitchen when I knocked, and was apologizing for her hand, which felt moist and floury as I took it in greeting. Her smile was frank, her laugh delightful, and I thought that any man could easily be bewitched by her.

"Martin's in his room. Why don't you go up and visit?"

I hesitated.

"Martin!" she called up the staircase.

"Well?"

"You've a visitor!" Her voice, although raised, lost none of its sweetness. "Shelby Ross is here to see you."

"Send him up!" Martin shouted in response.

"You'll stay for supper!" she said peremptorily.

Her name is Ellen, by the way, and if one were liable to falling in love, she would be a likely object of affection.

"Hello, Shelby!" cried Martin as I walked into his room. "I'm glad you stopped!"

I had been afraid of finding him morose or, worse, angry for my not having come to see him sooner. His expression, however, conveyed only a genuine pleasure at my visit.

"How are you?" I asked, determined to put behind me the upheaval of the previous night. "You look well."

"I feel well!"

I was unprepared for his jubilation; his mood could be called by no other name.

"Sit down!" he said. In his excitement, he spoke in the imperative.

I sat in a straight-backed chair by the window, through

which I could see your bridge, Roebling, towering above the rooftops. It is the presiding muse and judge of all who beetle about in the streets of lower Manhattan and Brooklyn.

"You seem uncommonly cheerful," I said, "for a man who's lost his toes."

"Not all of them, Shelby; I've enough left to be getting on with."

"Here. I bought you something."

I gave him *Clarel.* He glanced at it and offered a perfunctory "Thank you" before putting it aside. I was offended by his lack of interest in the gift but believed that I deserved no better. I realize now that my mind had been stained by the horrors of the Palace of Aladdin; its memory was a stain, which took the shape in my fancy of everything we consider monstrous.

"What's got you so excited, Martin?"

"While lying here, I thought of the most extraordinary plan!"

"What might that be?"

"To leave—"

"Leave?"

"—and go out west! I couldn't wait to tell you."

I should have realized that what he really hoped to leave was Gibbs, but I didn't then.

"And what will you do there? Dig for gold? Carry the Word into the wilderness and convert the savages? Join the cavalry and murder them? Or do you want to be a cowboy— or a cardsharp on a Mississippi riverboat?"

In the intoxication of his idea, he did not notice my

mockery. I couldn't see it, Roebling. He was too damned slender and refined. Why, he seemed to be verging on frailty! I still could not picture him in a native canoe on the Río de la Plata, where he'd been stricken with malaria.

"Martin, you were pulling my leg!"

"I'm perfectly serious."

"It takes money to emigrate, unless you intend to walk across the continent and live off the land like one of Sherman's 'bummers.'"

"I've got money saved," he said, unwilling to be put off by a joke. "I was saving for a trip to Italy to see the frescoes and whatnot. It was always my dream, Shelby, to travel for a while in the Old World. But I've decided to go west, young man! And you, my not-so-young friend, are going with me!"

He had spoken grandly and with such flourish that I could picture a cartouche in the air enclosing his fervent words—each sentence finishing in an exclamation mark.

"You must've lost your last wit lying here. Or did the sack hit you on the head after all?"

"If you'll be serious a moment, you'll see the beauty of it. We'll take the transcontinental to Frisco. I have an uncle there. He owns a small newspaper. I telegraphed him two days ago, and he immediately replied, 'Yes.'"

"'Yes' to what, exactly?"

"To our going out to work for him! You're not following very well, Shelby. You look like raw liver, by the way."

"I don't know anything about a newspaper, except how to read it, preferably with gloves on to keep my fingers clean."

"I'm going to be a reporter—I can write as well as the

next man. And you, Shelby, are going to manage the circulation. Any damn fool can do it!"

In his enthusiasm, he'd managed once again to offend me.

"The man whom you'll be replacing had a seizure last week and died."

"Undoubtedly from poor circulation."

He ignored my flippancy. "Don't you see? It was meant to be!"

I fell silent, picturing myself in San Francisco, managing the circulation. I admit the idea was not so preposterous as I'd first believed. Why *not* start again someplace new?

"We'll leave as soon as my foot's healed. What do you say?" He put out his hand. "Partners?"

I found myself clasping Martin's hand and saying, "I see nothing to stop us!" I had been swept away by the "beauty of it." Then I remembered that my means were slender, my savings nonexistent. "But I have no money of my own to speak of."

"I've enough to get us started. We'll need to be frugal— no Pullman car, champagne, buffalo tongue, and oysters."

No trousseau or wedding supper, I said to myself, and immediately shook my head to rid it of the thought. The "Imp of the Perverse" was thumbing its nose at me.

"We'll pack a few things and vamoose. Uncle Myer is sending tickets. He's even found a cheap hotel near the Presidio where we can flop till we get on our feet."

"Minus a few toes."

"Reporters don't write or type with their feet," he said, laughing.

"Do Franklin and Ellen know?"

"They think it's a grand idea! In fact, I promised to look around to see if I can find a typesetter's berth for Franklin. This city's going to the dogs."

After they had brought Boss Tweed home in handcuffs from Spain and locked him in Ludlow Street Jail, where he had the good sense to die of pneumonia, we thought to have seen the last of Tammany Hall and its henchmen. It didn't take Tweed's old cronies long to crown "Honest John" Kelly the new king of the dunghill. Not dogs, but rats have taken over the town, and the pickings are choice.

"Out there, we can make something of ourselves! We can make ourselves over."

"And Ellen?" I asked.

"She's the sort who can find a job anywhere."

"What does she do?"

In the space of the family's foyer and in the briefest of durations, she had captivated me. And why not? I'm a man like any other.

"She operates a Sholes typewriter."

That explained her hands, which were smooth and attractive, with nicely shaped nails. On the Eighth Avenue 'bus, I'd watched a young conductor flirt with another Irish girl. Her face, like Ellen's, was fair, and her hair ginger. She'd replied to his impertinences in a sweetly lilting voice, which nonetheless was capable of paying him back in kind. She was pretty, save for her hands, which looked boiled. I recognized them as belonging to a laundress.

"That is a highly desirable skill," I said earnestly.

"She's very good at her job. She works for a stenographic bureau. She's been typing manuscripts for Henry James while he's staying in New York."

The name Henry James meant nothing to me.

That evening with Ellen, Franklin, and Martin was one of the happiest in memory. My supper with the Melvilles could not hold a candle to it—no, not even if Herman in a temper had set fire to the tablecloth. Unlike that night, which had ended in rancor and, after too much drink, in stupefaction, the conversation on Maiden Lane was lively and amiable. The Finches were charming, and in that I can be charming, as well, I was able to hold my own. But they were far more cultivated than I, and when they got onto books, the theater, or the opera, I'd fiddle with my fork or tap my nose thoughtfully with a spoon.

Ellen noticed my discomfort and changed the subject to—of all things—baseball. The Finches were fanciers of this democratic pastime, which Walt Whitman praised. I marveled at them as they argued in the vernacular of the sport the merits of the new Metropolitan Club, the legality of the Reserve Clause, and the morality of Candy Cummings's skewball. On Saturday afternoons, in season, the three of them would ride the elevated train to 110th Street to watch the Metropolitans play the Gothams at the new Polo Grounds.

I handed round cigars—Ellen pretended to be hurt that I had not thought to bring her one—and we began to discuss our remove to San Francisco.

"Martin tells me you're in favor of it," I said, careful to

blow my cigar smoke toward the open window for fear of offending her.

"Very much so," she said, turning serious. "It will be good for him to get away from the city. We know he's been unhappy at the pier." She stopped and looked at me. I held her gaze, and she went on. "Uncle Myer will help him get started—and you, also, if you decide to go."

"We hope to join you as soon as we're able," said Franklin, holding his cigar at arm's length and squinting at the ember. "We're all eager to start a new life out there."

"Out there." He could have been talking about Outer Mongolia or one of Saturn's moons.

Martin beamed at one and then the other, and then all three of them turned their faces to me.

"I've made up my mind to go," I said, as if I were Napoléon announcing the invasion of Russia to his field marshals.

"Hooray!" cried Ellen.

"I'm glad to hear it," said Franklin. "I wouldn't feel right about letting my little brother go alone."

So I am to be a chaperone, I said to myself, watching Martin's face struggle between pleasure and embarrassment.

"Didn't I tell you?" asked Martin of them both. What he'd told them, he didn't say, but I guessed it had to do with our being friends.

Franklin poured four small glasses of brandy. We drank to one another; then he corked the bottle and returned it to the sideboard. There would be no drunken carousal that night.

ON THE OMNIBUS HOME to Mrs. McFadden's boarding-house, I became excited by the prospect of leaving everything behind me. In the Finches' kitchen, I had felt as if I were already becoming someone else—felt as devout Christians must after gnawing on the body of Christ. I could sense something clean and sweet beginning to transpire in me, as if a spring, long blocked by debris, had been made to flow again. Twice on the 'bus, I surprised myself and the other passengers with a bark of laughter, so very buoyant was my mood.

Lying in bed, I became aware, as if for the first time, of the odor of Mrs. McFadden's greasy cooking, the stink stealing into the room from the privy, and the sour smell of men who wash infrequently. My gut griped in protest. Soon, I told myself, you'll be standing in Golden Gate Park and breathing salt air born on the winds from the Pacific Ocean. In a month, we'll have put a continent between New York City and ourselves." Startled by my use of the most intimate of pronouns, I shook my head like a dog with a flea in its ear and waited for sleep to come. When it did, I was on board an opulent Pullman car, on a transcontinental train, which seemed to have no need of tracks. I was rushing toward the Mississippi and thence across the vast and unknowable American continent toward San Francisco, where the Orient begins and John Gibbs would hold no sway.

U. S. Grant's Home at 3 East Sixty-sixth Street, Near the Central Park, April 30, 1882

I was shown into the front room by the Irish housekeeper, whose insolent manner proclaimed her superiority to anyone who had business with a former president chiefly remembered for Black Friday, the Salary Grab, the Delano Affair, the Whiskey Ring, and other scandals that flourished during his administration, though not with his consent or knowledge. Grant had failed at almost everything he'd turned his hand to, except war, which chooses heroes and casualties according to the same eccentric law by which a fatal bullet finds one man and not another.

Everything in that room appears now with the stark clarity that memory will sometimes confer on the past. As he had during my previous visit, Grant sat slouched on a horsehair sofa, as if he were again astride his old warhorse Cincinnati. In the light of the window, I could see dust motes and wreathes of smoke rising from a cigar clamped in the mouth of a visitor who'd arrived before me. He was carelessly dressed in a white serge suit; his vest bore charred traces of tobacco embers. Around his neck, the general wore a piece of flannel smelling of liniment and camphor. He was suffering from a sore throat. He had an unlit cigar between his teeth and gave every indication of enjoying the stranger's tobacco smoke vicariously, and now and again, he would sniff deeply to give his nose the pleasure denied his mouth. I could see that it pained him to talk.

"General Grant."

"Mr. Ross."

"I hope I'm not intruding."

"Not at all." Grant turned to his other visitor and said, "Mr. Ross works for the Custom Service, alongside Melville."

"Glad to make your acquaintance, Mr. Ross," said the gentleman, who seemed more like an impersonator of one than the real McCoy.

"Please call me Shelby."

"Shelby, I wonder if you know Sam Clemens," said Grant, gesturing toward the other man, who was eyeing me shrewdly, as if estimating his chances of beating me at Indian arm wrestling. "He's better known to the public as Mark Twain."

"It's a pleasure, Mr. Twain—or Mr. Clemens, I should say," I replied, flustered. "A very great pleasure to make your acquaintance."

I had read *The Adventures of Tom Sawyer* and had seen in Tom something of my own youthful cunning and love of flimflam.

"Likewise," the author replied—gruffly, I thought. He blew more smoke into the room, so that my eyes began to water, and said, "Back before the war, I knew a man from Jackson County, Mississippi, who shared your Christian name."

"Is that a fact?" I asked, not interested in the coincidence, which was hardly remarkable.

I was there to see Grant, and although I admired the famous writer, I was impatient for him to leave. He showed no intention of doing so, however; instead, he settled in the arm chair and told a story whose preposterousness I considered a waste of the general's time and mine.

"He was a cardsharp on the *Cotton Blossom*. Curious fellow—not my sort of man at all. He affected an air of a gentleman gone to seed, who consoled himself with drink. He favored checkered waistcoats, yellow shoes, and bourbon muddled with bitters and sugar. In a pinch, he'd settle for a bottle of cheap rye just to show that, while he might have once belonged to a fine old family of the southern aristocracy, he had lately sunk down into the muck, where the common people live. He was a wizard at cards—none could beat him—and was universally despised for his luck at the table.

"During a game of faro, a man named Dolan, a coarse, ill-mannered type of person from Arkansas, pulled a bowie knife on Shelby and, faster than a ferret inside a lady's skirt, lopped off both his hands.

"Shelby scarcely turned a hair, and after the blood had been staunched with beefsteaks and his wrists tied off with fancy garters belonging to one of the 'soiled doves,' he took off his yellow shoes and socks and proceeded to deal with his toes. Damned if he didn't win the next three hands, though he hadn't any! The boys at the table commenced to grumble, and before Shelby knew it, he'd lost his toes to a small hatchet one of the gents had been hiding inside his coat. It didn't matter a particle to Shelby. The following night, he had himself wheeled into the card room by one of his lady friends. His face split wide open in a grin, he started to play cards with his teeth.

"Shelby cleaned out those gents—red-faced and bilious in defeat—about as quick as a plate of oysters disappears down the necks of visitors to a house of ill repute or pennies from a collection plate passed among Bowery Boys. The mood at the table grew tense, like a frog in the vicinity of a python or a negro at a Klan convention. A feller who'd lost his pants, so to speak, happened to be a traveling dentist. He kept his instruments close to his vest, and in the time it takes to say good-bye, he'd pulled Shelby's teeth right out of his head. Witnesses to the atrocity claimed they made a sound like a keel scraping over a gravelly shoal or else lake ice cracking in a thaw. I've got one of Shelby's gold-filled molars on my watch chain; it makes an interesting fob and a provocative topic when conversation stalls." Clemens hauled his watch out of his vest pocket by the chain, whose fob was a tiny riverboat carved in ivory. "It must be on my other chain."

"What did he do next?" I asked politely, for I saw that Grant was enjoying the yarn.

"Who?" Scratching his chin, Clemens pretended to have lost the thread.

"Shelby the cardsharp!" barked Grant, causing the flannel wrap to give up an aromatic ghost of liniment to the rancid atmosphere.

"He quit cards and became a Transcendentalist."

I didn't see the joke, but Grant guffawed.

"Somebody open the goddamn window!" he croaked. "It stinks like dirty feet in here."

I jumped up and opened the window. On Sixty-sixth Street, a teamster was beating his horse.

"Thank you kindly, Shelby."

"A name can mark a man. Like Ulysses here, who has arrived home at last to the patient Julia, his Penelope, after the wars and strife of public life. Do you find it burdensome to carry a name fit for an allegory, Mr. President, sir?"

"Horseshit!" whinnied Grant.

"I'm not so sure about that, U.S. If a man has a handle, such as you'd encounter in a made-up story, he might come to think of himself as a figment of some damned storyteller's imagination. He might believe he doesn't exist in the real world at all."

Clemens ground his spent cigar into the dirt of the fernery beside his chair and then gave me a look such as an owl would give a mouse. "Now take *his* moniker." He cocked a thumb at me. "It could only belong to a cardsharp or an ephebe."

"You've poked enough fun at Shelby for one afternoon!" admonished Grant.

"There's something prophetic about it," said Clemens, ignoring his friend.

"I don't follow you." I was getting more and more irritated.

Ignoring my vexation, Clemens snuffled, took out a handkerchief, snuffled again for good measure, and said, "Shelby—" He sneezed, blew his nose emphatically, examined his handkerchief, and, like a bad actor playing the blind soothsayer Tiresias, finished his thought: "Shall be—*what*?

Another panic? Another civil war? Certainly not an age of peace."

"I doubt it," said Grant, speaking with curious solemnity, as though he had glimpsed the future and found it a cold and desolated place.

"It makes me feel kind of jumpy being in the same room with you, Shelby," said Clemens, combing his scraggly mustache. "I'd hate to get tangled in one of your prophecies. What a man can't see won't hurt him, but I've a feeling that if I were to peer into your bloodshot eyes, I'd see myself in a place where the only smoking a man gets to do is when he's roasting his backside over hellfire."

"Shelby, what have you to say for yourself?" wheezed Grant, who was again amused.

"General, I have no idea what he's talking about."

I didn't care for Clemens, who was as cruel to me as Huck Finn had been to Jim.

"Friend of Melville's, you say?" asked Clemens.

"We work together in the West Street customs office."

"*Hmmm.* You're sure you're not a literary fellow?" he asked suspiciously.

"Heaven forbid!"

"Heaven doesn't seem to have much say in the matter. Seems like we're up to our eyes in literary types, not to mention literati, lyceums, and critics. Hardly anybody's taking up an honest profession these days. Even the old-time gunfighters are selling their memoirs to the penny dreadfuls." He glanced sharply at Grant, who ignored him.

"I've tried honest professions and dishonest ones," I said

flippantly. "But I'd rather shovel shit with a fork than be a writer."

Clemens nodded, as if I'd said something wise. "I've been trying all afternoon to get Grant to let me publish his memoirs. He's not a writer; therefore, he's a man whom we can safely turn loose with pen and paper."

"I don't have a memoir to publish!" growled the old man.

"You'd be surprised how quickly you'd have one if only you'd make a start. Writing is nothing more than knitting—one strand is truth, the other embellishment."

Grant snorted and chewed his unlit cigar.

"Only great men and women can be forgiven their immodesty in having written their memoirs." Clemens turned to me and asked, "Did you happen to see our friend's piece on Shiloh in *Century Magazine*?"

"No, I didn't."

"The facts were illuminating, even if the literary style was dry as hardtack. If you set your mind to it, I know damned well you can write me the story of your life, Hiram. If you could take Vicksburg while you were drunk, you can write a picayune reminiscence."

"I wasn't drunk!" said Grant peevishly. "I had a migraine."

A man with a headache ain't half so interesting to the public as an old army soak!"

"What brings you here, Mr. Ross?" asked Grant, hoping to change the subject.

I had gone to see the general for obscure reasons. I told myself I would tell him of my decision to emigrate and ask his advice. But there was no reason why he should care to give it. We'd spoken only once before, and that briefly. Then suddenly I realized that I'd gone there to set the record straight. I needed to unburden myself of the lie I'd told for so long, I had come at last to believe it. During my stay in Sing Sing, I would have time to ponder the meaning of my visit to East Sixty-sixth Street and recognize it as the stirring of conscience, which had lain dormant in whatever bodily organ it resides. I wanted to square myself with my fellow men and—an even more self-important notion— with history, which Grant represented as well as any other Caliban of our ignoble age. I wanted to make a clean break with New York City and the past.

"General, I want to apologize."

He appeared perplexed by my declaration and even more by the earnestness with which I had uttered it.

Out of the corner of my eye, I saw Clemens lean forward expectantly. "Apologize for what, Shelby?" he asked. His unruly mustache twitched in anticipation of a shameful admission.

I ignored him and spoke directly to the general.

"The last time I was here, I lied about having fought in the war. I did no such thing. My father hired a substitute."

"You're damned lucky to have been kept out of it!" barked Grant hoarsely. "'Only the defeated and deserters go to the wars' is what Thoreau had to say on the subject of patriotism, which he called 'a maggot in the brain.'"

"'If the bubble reputation can be obtained only at the cannon's mouth, I am willing to go there for it, provided the cannon is empty,'" remarked Clemens, quoting himself with a saturnine air, which would send paying audiences into fits of laughter.

"If everybody who claims to have fought at Gettysburg had truly done so, there'd have been hardly room to swing a cat. Men would have been packed into the real estate like pickles in a jar or herring in a barrel."

"Hiram, that's the kind of salt to flavor a tasteless dish of reminiscence!" cried Clemens approvingly.

"Goddamn it, Sam, don't call me 'Hiram!'" Incensed, Grant's ragged voice had nearly formed itself into a shout, such as had hectored the Union troops at the Cumberland to take Fort Donelson from the rebels. Overnight, he'd become the darling of the Union newspapers, which gave him the nickname "Unconditional Surrender" Grant.

He'd been christened "Hiram Ulysses," Melville said after our March visit, but an Ohio congressman mistook the name when he nominated him for admission to West Point. "U.S. Grant" stuck for the remainder of his life. And by this name, acquired by a misunderstanding, he became identified, personally, with the Union he fought to preserve and unwittingly betrayed.

"Will you get off your high horse, *Hiram*, and give me some meat to publish? I invested my shirt and my back teeth in Paige's infernal typesetting machine. It's got more parts than a mule and is just as stubborn. I doubt the good Lord Himself could have managed, in twice the time He spent on His creation, to contrive a more complicated piece of machinery, not excepting Eve. I've lost so much money on that goddamn compositor, I've had to go into the publishing business to keep it fed, and my family starved. Publishing is only a little higher in the scheme of things than a flea circus, and a publisher is held in the same esteem as a congressmen or a floosy, both of whom will turn a man's pockets inside out the minute his eyes are closed."

"I'll give it some thought," replied Grant, who looked as if he'd been run over twice by a brewery wagon. "Now, gentlemen, if you'll forgive me, it's time for my nap."

"I'll be back to bully you some more," said Clemens kindly.

"Get the hell out of here, you no-good son of a bitch Johnny Reb!"

Clemens had spent two weeks in the Confederate army before lighting out for Nevada Territory to prospect for silver, which he didn't find.

"Shelby," said Grant as I was preparing to leave. "I wouldn't waste time thinking about that other matter if I were you. Give my regards to Melville. Tell him I'm enjoying his poems."

The old man put his feet up on the sofa and shut his eyes. We left him to his nap.

"He's right," said Clemens. "The pangs of conscience are no worse than hunger, which can be appeased with a twenty-five-cent piece." He broke into a boyish grin, and his mordancy was dissipated, like Angostura bitters stirred in a glass of gin. "Mr. Ross, I happen to have a pocketful of quarters—a grubstake for liquor and a free lunch at McSorley's."

I decided to accompany Clemens. If the ale house had once served to quench Abraham Lincoln's thirst, it could mine, as well. As we walked down Lexington, I wondered what I had hoped to accomplish by visiting the general.

McSorley's Ale House at 15 East Seventh Street, April 30, 1882

Clemens wanted to have a drink among the Irish, so that he could count his lucky stars he'd had the good sense to be born with scotch running though his veins.

"Mostly, my ancestors were Cornish, who drank whatever they could smuggle or was washed up on the beach from a ship they'd wrecked," he said after wiping beer foam from his shaggy mustache. "Terrible lot of sinners come from Cornwall!"

"You were hard on the general," I said brusquely. I had felt a grievance coming out like a rash during the elevated ride to the Lower East Side.

"You mustn't mind what I said. God and Grant know what I think of him. The poor man has always had a hard-scrabble life. He was a fine president: He outlawed the Klan, came down on the carpetbaggers, and pushed the Fifteenth Amendment through a congress of jackasses. He fought for freedmen's rights at a time when one half of the population wanted to lynch the other. And contrary to public opinion, which comes as near the truth about as often as Halley's Comet does earth, he was not a drunkard. The soldiers loved him, and soldiers won't follow a drunkard into the Valley of the Shadow of Death—leastwise not when they're sober."

He picked at a tooth with his fingernail and said, "My mouth tastes of smoke and cinders. I'm not sure God meant us to ride in trains two stories above the street, although the view was breathtaking. I could count the number of Chinese cigar rollers and Hebrew rag pickers that can fit in a tiny tenement-house room."

He downed his beer, as if to flush the modern world from his system, including James Paige's diabolical typesetter, which was ruining him. He banged his empty schooner on the bar and called for another.

"How is life in the customhouse?"

"Not much of one," I replied. "I'm moving to San Francisco."

"Frisco will be the making of you. Broad, wholesome, and charitable views of human beings cannot be acquired by vegetating in a corner all one's life," he declared, fixing an eye on the proceedings behind the bar.

The landlord, an oily man whose nearly identical height and girth made him tend toward the spherical, had just sliced the foam from a beer glass with a paddle and was setting it proudly before Clemens as if he'd cut the Koh-i-Noor diamond. Having embarked on a third whiskey, I was beginning to grow fond of the curmudgeon, whose obstreperous hair looked like the snakes of Medusa.

"I'm worried about that throat of his," said Clemens, showing genuine concern for his friend.

"Too many cigars."

"The trouble with Grant is his heart! You wouldn't know it to look at him, Shelby, but he's a sweet old crust. I've known him to be downright sentimental when he's drunk—though he is not a drunkard! Not every man who drinks is a sot, any more than every man who fiddles is Nero or one of them Strauss fellas."

Clemens dipped a finger in his beer and, revolving it on the rim of his glass, produced a note, weird and sostenuto, which was once thought to drive women mad. It reminded me of the sound of a fingernail on slate or a tune played on a saw. A dog lying on the sawdust floor began to whine pitiably.

"That'll be enough of that, gent, or I'll stick that glass where you'll never see it again!" growled a big burly fellow with pig's bristles on his chin—a stevedore or a carter by the look of him.

"I'm sorry you have no ear for music, sir."

Infuriated, the man leaned across me and grabbed Clemens by the lapel of his white suit.

Clemens called to the landlord, who was gathering up bottles in his beefy arms, as if they were his children. "Mr. McSorley, I presume."

"The name's Hannigan," said the man with the bottles.

"Mr. Shenanigans, is this not the amateur musical society, and haven't I been invited to entertain with my glass harmonica?"

"It is not, and you have not!" replied an indignant Hannigan.

"It seems, then, that I have made a mistake—not the first, nor in all likelihood the last. My apologies, and God's blessing on you all! Good sir, if you will let go of my lapel, I'll stand you to a drink of Jameson or the noble Bushmills. I would also like a dish of ale drawn for the dog, whose ears I have unwittingly offended."

The man let go. Clemens smoothed the rumpled fabric of his coat.

"A great pity that I left my Ancient Order of Hibernians pin on my other coat. It would have prevented this misunderstanding between friends, not forgetting man's best friend, whose slumbers I disturbed."

The Irishman thought it better to accept the whiskey and remove himself to the other end of the bar rather than prolong a discussion with a lunatic.

"One for me and for my friend," said the imperturbable comedian to the landlord, who by now had returned the bottles to the shelf, above which lolled a painted lady dressed in feathers.

Roebling, I couldn't decide whether I ought to be afraid or amused.

"You baited a man who could have cracked your skull."

"It's a terrible bully I am!" replied Clemens with a comical lilt to a voice that, as a rule, tended southerly in its intonation. "Sitting here among the mackerel snappers, I'm reminded of one of Nast's lampoons, entitled 'The Usual Irish Way of Doing Things.' He'd drawn a soused Paddy lighting a cigar while he sits on a powder keg. Nast's pen is sharp enough to draw blood from an elephant."

I started at a muffled explosion, but it was only a cork being pulled from a bottle.

The barroom quieted as each man drank toward forgetfulness, insofar as the coins in his pockets allowed.

"Grant's broke," said Clemens. "That son of a bitch Ward cleaned him out."

The general had had the misfortune or naïveté to surround himself with crooks. Now in his old age, he'd sunk $100,000 into his son's brokerage firm. In collusion with the bank, Ferdinand Ward, his son's partner, had bought a small fortune in stocks, putting up as collateral not only the firm's assets but also its clients' securities—identical securities for multiple purchases. Grant had reached the end of the rope with which a man will pull himself out of the quicksand or hang himself.

"Being an honorable cuss, he's determined to repay every last debt."

"Can his memoirs save him?" I asked, with the humility of someone whose mistrust in a fellow human has proved false.

"I don't see any other way for Julia to escape a poverty that wouldn't even qualify as genteel."

"And the general?"

Clemens shook his head sadly. "Not long for this world. But I'll be damned if he leaves it from a bed in the poorhouse!"

Clemens tapped thoughtfully on the bar with his nail. "Sometimes I don't know who I am: Sam Clemens, Mark Twain, Tom Sawyer, or an invention of Charles Dickens—Wilkins Micawber, with a Missouri drawl and a habit of irritating his fellow man."

He fell silent, and I noticed how the noise of the world outside on the crowded street and pavement flooded into the taproom, like the roar of an ocean slamming into a stone jetty. I had an intimation of something—a premonition—an inkling of dread. I couldn't guess its cause, but I felt it all the same.

"The tide of humanity will drown us all," I said with the tentativeness of a man who has told a dubious joke. Clemens ignored it, and I felt my face flush in embarrassment. Well, I had been guilty of worse folly. I'd been to the school of humiliation and had learned to eat my words and humble pie. I laughed queerly to give my mouth something to do.

"Who are you?" asked Clemens, looking askance at me. "Do you even know yourself?"

I gazed into a mirror hanging between the nude woman, whose throat had been painted in the rosy tones of typhoid fever, and a foxed and fly-specked calendar, where time had stopped for the Irish on March 5, 1867, the day of the Fenian Rising. I wondered at the stranger whose face I saw reflected there.

"So you're lighting out for the territories. Well, I wish you luck."

"I'm going to be a newspaperman."

"God help us!"

Roebling's Second-Story Room on Brooklyn Heights, May 17, 1884

You'd have thought I was a boy impatient for Saturday afternoon, when, having finished my chores, I could go out into the street and play cowboys and Indians. As I waited for

Martin's foot to mend, I felt happier than I'd been since the panic pulled the rug out from under me. Needless to say, the rug had been hand-knotted in Persia; its replacement was made of rags stitched to old sacking. Each time I visited Martin, I would take a small gift for Ellen: a lace handkerchief; a card of whalebone buttons; an African totem carved from ebony, found in the hold of a Portuguese merchant ship; a Waterman pen bought in a moment of extravagance at a stationer's on University Place; and a packet of seeds with which to grow forget-me-nots, about which Thoreau had observed that "even flowers must be modest."

"I do believe that you are courting me, Mr. Ross!" she said, her pretty eyes glinting with mischief.

I denied it, my cheeks flaming.

"Yes, you are!" she teased. "I'm flattered by your attentiveness nearly enough to run away with you. But then who would cook Franklin's dinner, and, more important, who would type Mr. James's novels? You may care nothing for a husband's broken heart, but you mustn't think to deprive an illustrious novelist of a neatly typed manuscript!"

I sighed—romantically, I hoped.

Why shouldn't I flirt with her? My experience with women may have been slight, but I'm as interested as the next man in what hides beneath a woman's skirts! Ellen didn't take me seriously, but neither did she take me for a fool.

I returned the copy of *Redburn* to the Mercantile Library for Martin and borrowed Mark Twain's *Roughing It*, a book with Bret Harte's story "The Luck of Roaring

Camp," and Ambrose Bierce's *Nuggets and Dust Panned Out in California*. The temporary invalid feasted on these western tales and loved to recount them, as he had told me Melville's sea stories, until I grew sick of them. His feelings hurt, he would sulk when I grumbled or dozed in the chair. For the most part, I shared his excitement, and we'd spend hours making lists of "bare necessities," drawing up itineraries, and talking about our life at the other end of America. Tired and restless, I would go home to bed and count the days until I could leave it and Gansevoort Pier for good. Neither Martin nor I mentioned John Gibbs.

I had intended to keep our plan a secret but succumbed to an overmastering desire to disclose it not only to Melville, who cheered us, but also to Gibbs, the chief reason for our wish to leave New York. The most inexplicable perversity is that a man will sometimes put his own head into the noose. To my surprise, Gibbs shook my hand, clapped me on the back, and wished me luck. He's glad to be getting rid of me, I thought, so as not to be constantly reminded of his disgrace by a witness to it.

"To celebrate your fresh start in California, I want to give you a treat tonight—something to remember me by," he said, smiling broadly enough to make me wince at the sight of his black gums and rotted teeth. He had all the appurtenances of a stage villain in a melodrama except the waxed mustache.

I shuddered, and he evidently mistook the cause of my repulsion. Even now, two years later, I wonder how a man of such obvious depravity could have *worked* me. In prison,

I sometimes felt a strange sensation, as though the world were dissolving. Then I would think—I could easily think it now—that you and I, John Gibbs, Martin Finch, Ellen, Franklin, the bridge outside the window are figments! Of Melville's! He has the brain for such fantasies.

"I promise, Shelby, the treat I have in mind is nothing like the Slide!" He laughed. "You must have been shocked! But don't worry; your secret is safe with me." He winked in that lewd way of his. "What I propose for this evening is a trip to West Houston Street to see the fights."

I had no wish to go.

"You must let me do this!" he said insistently. "To make up for that unfortunate night." He could sense my reluctance and began to press the matter artfully. "Unless blood sports make you squeamish."

I did not want him to think me lacking in manliness, which in our time is measured by the strength of a man's passion for cock- and dogfights and the gory sight of blood spurting from another man's battered nose.

I agreed to accompany him. What else could I have done? I promised myself that it would be the last night I'd ever spend in his company.

Harry Hill's Saloon in West Houston Street, the Bowery, May 5, 1882

Harry Hill is celebrated for his wealth and notorious for the manner of its accumulation. Horse dealer, brawler, gambler, unsavory entrepreneur, and bare-knuckle boxing promoter, he counted among his friends both criminals and politicians, who patronized his saloons. His barroom in the Bowery was a den of iniquity—forgive the worn phrase; it's the only one in my glossary that is apt. As I'd soon discover, bare-knuckle boxing is a far cry from fisticuffs between gentlemen. It is— Have you ever seen a match, Roebling?

You've missed nothing that can't be seen when a butcher feeds pig meat into a sausage grinder.

No sooner had we sat down at a table ringed with the sticky imprints of beer glasses than Gibbs grew excited. The atmosphere of that suffocating room seemed to send him into a rapture. He nosed it, as if a fragrant vintage had been placed before him. Momentarily, he forgot me, and I considered sidling out from the table and getting away. The stink of the West Street holding pens and slaughterhouses would have been preferable to that foul hole. For a second time, I had let myself be brought to a place where men debase themselves. I had put myself into the hands of my mortal enemy, who wanted only to humiliate me. Thus do some men seem bent on self-destruction.

Harry Hill took the stage, which doubled for a ring, to raucous applause, hoots, and gibes in the colorful vernacular of the Five Points and Sailors Town. He announced the first act in the night's brutal comedy—an "Irish Stand Down" fought between square-jawed Colin O'Neil and a square-headed Prussian, whose name was lost in a gust of anti-German sentiments.

You're not familiar with the term?

That speaks well of you. An Irish Stand Down, I was informed by my escort through the underworld, sweating beside me in a rabid heat of anticipation, is a contest between two men in which they punch each other, turn by turn again, accepting the blows without moving their feet, which soon become mired in blood and human slurry.

"I was at the fight when Ben Haight went eight hours in the ring against Bill Murphy before he quit," said Gibbs, licking his lips. "What a mess they made of each other!"

Two men entered from the wings, to use a theatrical metaphor, as if words could alter the hideous actuality of the spectacle. They were as unlike the pugilists I had watched at Madison Square Garden as mongrels are from the fancy dogs at the Westminster Kennel Club.

The men were brutishly built and moved without grace or efficiency. Their prowess lay solely in their ability to stand and absorb blows to the face and abdomen. That they could do so for hours only confirmed the impression one had that they were of an order of being akin to a granite column or a sack of feed. It was difficult for me to watch and nearly impossible to pity them—although I knew poverty had made them fight—any more than I could pity a stone I'd kicked in frustration.

Gibbs appeared on the verge of unconsciousness, so enthralled was he by the combat. The fighters wore only loincloths in the style of ancient Greek wrestlers, and in the glare of the limelight, their flesh shone. We were sitting close enough to smell the mingled odors of blood and sweat, which Gibbs savored as a gourmand would sweetbreads or a calf's brain sautéed in black butter. Revolted, I shut my eyes on the jellied faces of the Irishman and the German and, worse, on the shiny faces of the other spectators. I'd seen them before in theaters where women undressed, as if for human sacrifice, while men leaned expectantly toward the little stage, their countenances transmogrified by lust.

The Irishman and the German continued to exchange blows, until I could no longer stand the sight of them.

"I'm feeling sick," I told Gibbs. "I need air."

He turned his face to mine and scowled; at the same time, he grabbed my arm to stay me. He said something, but his words were lost in a din punctuated rhythmically by the unspeakable sound of bare fists on flesh. For a moment, I thought I saw hatred in his smoke-reddened eyes, and I grew afraid. He smiled—because he saw my fear? Who can say? But he relented and let go of my arm and, bringing his lips close to my ear, said, "So you're squeamish after all." He patted the back of my hand and nodded toward the door to the street. As I was making my way through the jostling crowd of onlookers, I glanced back at the ring in time to see the German fall.

Gibbs took my arm and led me down the street until the air revived me. We stopped at a taproom that gave every appearance of being a favorite haunt of stevedores, road menders, and sailors caught on land and waiting to return again to their natural element. Gibbs was clearly in his element, while I felt like a mouse dropped by the tail into a snake pit for the amusement of the public.

We drank a whiskey each, and then Gibbs urged a glass of absinthe on me. I rarely drink it, not caring for the taste of anise and sweet fennel, but once again, I seemed to be in thrall to strange impulses.

"Some call it 'the green fairy,'" he said, licking his spoon after having dissolved a sugar cube in the pale green spirit. "It makes me forget myself."

I could guess what there was in him that needed to be forgotten.

The room tilted to starboard and then, having briefly righted itself, listed in the opposite direction. Melville had walked on decks lurching like this floor—filthy beyond belief—as he sailed toward the cannibal isles. I was pleased with myself and hoped to remember the comparison in the morning so that I could impress him with my cleverness.

Men moved about, encircling me like trash eddying on a dirty river. Their mouths were slashes, their eyes embers, their lips snakes writhing around a hole. Where was God in all this wreckage? I would have asked myself had I had my wits about me. As if in answer to my unspoken and scarcely formulated question, I felt a hand inside my vest, and thinking it was Gibbs, I shoved him off his stool.

"Goddamn you, Ross! I'll make you sorry you were ever born!" A fury mounted in him, like fire in dry tinder.

"Somebody had his hand inside my coat," I said. My words staggered drunkenly.

"The place is famous for pickpockets," replied Gibbs, my answer having satisfied him. "Has someone lifted your purse?"

I patted my vest, felt the wallet's bulge, and said, "I have it."

Gibbs gathered up our drinks and elbowed me toward an empty table at the back.

"We can talk in private here," he said, setting down our glasses.

I knew enough not to drink any more. Intent on his tête-à-tête, Gibbs didn't notice my abstinence.

"What do you want?" I asked, planting my elbows on the table to keep my head from falling forward. Someone else had asked me that question. Who could it have been?

"Tonight you've seen the world," he said. "Believe it or not, Shelby, this is *your* world—you belong to it. I've studied you, and I know you—know your heart. You are one of us."

His words came at me. They enveloped me like drizzle—a yellow rain. What does he mean? I asked myself.

"I must go," I said, feeling caught like a minnow in a net. I tried to stand but fell back in my chair. Gibbs took my hand, and once again I shuddered. He ignored the tremor, or else he misinterpreted it. I attempted to stand again.

"Sit!" he commanded.

I tried to focus my eyes on his face, but they refused to stay put, searching the dark corners of the room instead.

"You are not going to California," he said softly.

"No?"

"No. Your place is here."

I had no idea what "here" meant to him, unless it was this odious barroom.

"I know what you've been up to with your friend."

"My friend?"

I couldn't make any sense of it, Roebling.

"Martin Finch, or should I call him Mary Finch?"

Before I could gather my thoughts in order to protest, he had gone on. "In some men, it is an abomination, in others not. You have a womanish temperament, Shelby. It's true—you know it is—deny it as much as you like." His voice was sad. "No, you cannot go to California with Martin Finch."

"You don't understand," I blurted. "Martin and I are—"

He leaned toward me and hissed, "Sodomites!"

I jerked back in my chair, appalled.

"It's not true!"

The trouble lies in words, Roebling. There is none for what Walt Whitman, unashamed and innocent, gloried in. We call it "sodomy," "bestiality," and "abomination" because we have no others, and what we call it prejudices the mind and strikes balefire against a flinty heart; in conflagrations like that are books and witches burned.

"Martin is a cannibal. And as surely as Eliza Donner ate the arm of Samuel Shoemaker by Alder Creek, he will have you."

I looked on him aghast and completely sobered, though my legs still balked.

"You're wrong about him!"

"Let's say you were unaware of Martin's unnatural interest in you."

Again I started to object, but he would not brook interruption.

"If you aren't guilty of gross indecency, then he must be. Is he?"

I struggled to find words to make a suitable reply and

put an end to this absurdity, but his voice, modulating from irritability to patient sympathy, went on and on.

"Is he? Is he? Is he?"

"No! No! No!"

"Are you unnatural?"

"I am not!" I shouted.

"Of course not, Shelby! It's Martin who's the bugger."

I shook my head wearily. I wanted to lay my head on the tabletop. I thought of the long way home to bed. However will I get there? I wondered. It's miles and miles from here, and the hour is late. The effort it would take to get up from the chair, walk out onto the street, find a horsecar, and ride to McFadden's boardinghouse seemed immense. The journey home would be as exhausting as a trip to California, or China. No, I couldn't do it, couldn't move my legs in my weariness. I felt as you must have, Roebling, when the bends took you and made you bedfast.

"I found this among his things," said Gibbs, solemnly producing evidence in the trial of poor Martin.

He set a disgusting photograph in front of me.

"Among—his—things?" I stammered. It was beyond belief. "You're a liar!"

"Am I?"

I glared at him.

He shrugged. Roebling, the man shrugged his shoulders lightly, as if he'd lost a half-dollar in a game of three-card monte!

He got up from the table and left. Without another

word! I stared for a moment at the photograph, then angrily tore it up.

Why have I become the object of such inhuman attention? I asked myself. Is it Gibbs's revenge for my having struck him or for any airs and graces that I might have retained from my better days? Is he enraged by the thought of guileless affections between men—or does he crave them? Is it desire or shame that goads him? Or is he Iago after all, whose motives were pure—that is, unadulterated by either reason or unreason. Iago was Iago because he could be no other; likewise, Gibbs must be Gibbs.

The Central Park, May 7, 1882

On Sunday, I felt obliged to visit Martin.

No, not to confront him with Gibbs's accusation, which I didn't believe. The reason had nothing to do with Gibbs. Martin and I had things to discuss about our remove to San Francisco. His foot was nearly healed; we could leave New York within the week. There were a few details to finalize, and then we could be off.

"Hello, Franklin," I said when he answered my knock on the door.

"Morning, Shelby! Come in."

He is a genial and good-natured man, as brawny and awkward as his younger brother was lithe.

"I need to talk to Martin," I said.

"He's asleep. He had a visitor last night who appeared to upset him. After the fellow left, I could hear Martin moving about his room till daylight."

The compass needle in my head swung round, until it stopped at the image of John Gibbs, a human lodestone that could attract by his loathsomeness. The compulsion is shared by dogs, which will sniff delicately at their own filth, and by readers whose finer feelings are overcome by morbid curiosity about stories like those by Edgar Poe. I've had the same unwholesome feeling when gazing at a poor freak of nature in a sideshow tent. I recall a mermaid on display in Hester Street, near East Broadway, purported to have been hauled up from the depths of the Tyrrhenian Sea by Corsican fishermen. Melville took me to see it—or her; the gender of pronouns can be misleading when fantastic beings are concerned.

"What did he look like?" I asked Franklin, fairly certain of his answer.

"Squat and well built; looked to be fifty or so. He said he works with Martin on the pier."

Gibbs!

"I'll just have a word with Martin."

"Let him sleep, Shelby."

"Yes," I said, checking an impulse to hurry up the stairs.

Ellen sailed into the front room, a favorable wind at her back, so to speak.

"Good morning, Mr. Ross!" she greeted me brightly. "We're off to the Central Park. Why don't you come with us?"

"There's a thought!" said Franklin agreeably.

You wouldn't be agreeable, Franklin, if you knew I coveted your wife! (The penitent, who has the hairy ear of a priest to fill, finds that his minor sins are easily remembered, whereas matters of grave consequence to the soul are told reluctantly, if at all.)

"I'd love to!" I said, happy to forget Gibbs—and Martin—for an afternoon.

Franklin took the wicker hamper Ellen had packed, and we walked to Battery Place station to take the Ninth Avenue elevated. Boarding a northbound train, I was in high spirits and admitted to myself without a shred of guilt that I was happier in Ellen and Franklin's company than I would have been in Martin's.

RIDING ABOVE NINTH AVENUE, I glimpsed the Elysian Fields, next to the river in Hoboken, where the Metropolitans play.

"A splendid name for a baseball field!" said Ellen. "And to think that when it was one of the Fortunate Isles, at the western edge of the earth, it belonged to Cronos and not New Jersey!"

The house and building fronts below the tracks had also become vulgarized by cast-iron facades painted in imitation of building stone.

I know you despise them, Roebling. Lies are detestable, whether expressed in words, paint, iron, brick, or stone.

We left the steam train at the Eighty-sixth Street station and walked to the park entrance known as Mariner's Gate. We strolled amid flowering dogwood and tulip trees across the green sward to the lake at Seventy-eighth. A few blocks to the south, the city's impoverished folk found respite from their drudgery in Sheep Meadow, if they had scraped together the pennies for the horsecar or el ride from the foul tenements, where the water is not so clean as it was in the old Piggery. Harsenville and the Piggery District had been home to poor negro, Irish, and German families, until they were evicted to make way for Olmstead's democratic Eden. (Eminent domain is only Manifest Destiny in miniature.) The sheep were happier, as they grazed on the meadow's rich grass, unaware of their privileged life inside the park, safe from the knife of Abraham or a West Street market butcher.

While Franklin and I lounged on a tartan blanket, which smelled faintly of camphor flakes, Ellen unpacked the hamper of bread, cheese, and wine and talked about Paris because, she said, the picture we three made reminded her of Manet's *The Luncheon on the Grass*, which she had seen in a book belonging to Henry James. She smiled coyly and asked me if I'd ever seen a reproduction of the painting.

"I don't believe so."

"It's one you would remember, Mr. Ross!"

She laughed, as pleased as a child who has said something naughty.

"I don't much care for the French," I said with a patrician sniff of disdain.

"Mr. James would be shocked to hear it!" said Ellen, pretending to be horrified.

Although there were no sheep to be seen in the better purlieu of the park, she recited a poem about a shepherd.

Franklin, the tip of his tongue showing, whittled a stick. I lay on my back and chewed a stem of sweet grass. Unwittingly, we'd assembled into a pastoral tableau of three rustics on a holiday.

> Amidst her cheeks the rose and lily strive,
> Lily snow-white:
> When their contend doth make their colour thrive,
> Colour too bright
> For shepherd's eyes.

"What fun to be picnicking with two handsome swains!" she then said, taking off her straw hat.

Again I marveled at her hair, whose color and fineness resembled strands of copper wire.

On such a day as this, I told myself, twenty-year-old Herman Melville began his first sea voyage, as a cabin boy sailing from Coenties Slip to Liverpool aboard the *St. Lawrence*. Could he have foreseen the disaster of his second voyage on the whaleship *Acushnet*, his desertion, his badly infected leg, his convalescence among the "roistering blades of savages," the menace of the cannibals, the fear and hunger, would he have left in a carefree mood or done the sensible thing and gone into business, like his everlastingly debt-ridden father?

Would *your* father, Roebling, have begun the bridge had he known that, by a chance concatenation of events, it would kill him? Would you have taken on his work knowing what suffering would befall you? And if that afternoon in the Central Park, I had foreseen the coming disaster, would

I have hurried to the nearest train and fled the city? Sometimes I wonder if the story had not already been written.

By Melville, yes. When I finished his novel *Redburn*, I could imagine myself having been trapped in a lurid story with John Gibbs.

"Shelby, where will you be next month this time?" asked Ellen thoughtfully.

Martin and I had often plotted our new beginning, and I could reply without hesitation. "In a rooming house at the top of Russian Hill, with a view of San Francisco Bay. The windows are open. I'm lying on my bed after managing Uncle Myer's circulation. Seen distantly through the window, a steamer is bound for the Galápagos, where tortoises lie sleeping inside an ancient dream."

Ellen looked at me appreciatively, and for a moment, I imagined her with me in that room. Each of us is architect and chief engineer of our dreams, Roebling, and they can be as difficult to build, the materials as refractory, the reasons against them as sound, the risks as great, and their realization as well-nigh impossible as they are in a feat of civil engineering.

Ellen and I walked along the lake, and she told me of her happiness. The words came easily as though she were describing an outing on Coney Island. I envied her, and I envied Franklin for having had the good fortune to marry her. I was dreaming, don't you see? I could have been a shepherd, and she a shepherdess in a pastoral poem by Theocritus.

We sat on a rustic bench conceived in the mind of Frederick Law Olmstead and not in an ancient Greek's. We looked at the water, where a stately pair of swans was gliding for no other reason than to confirm our Sunday's idyll. A collie dog ran into the water, attracted by the magnetic force of a stick thrown by a boy; the imperturbable swans moved just beyond reach of the dog's commotion.

"Isn't it wonderful, Shelby?" asked Ellen, squeezing my hand.

Phoebe, I said to myself; I am your Silvius. How wonderful a dream can sometimes be! And how very terrible.

I had boarded an el train in lower Manhattan, only to step out into a play or an opera. I wouldn't have been surprised if Ellen had begun to sing an aria to the trumpeting of the swans and the barking of the dog and the bewilderment of the boy. For the space of the afternoon, the world and all its sordidness had fallen away, leaving only the park, two of the three Finches, and me. If only it could have continued!

Do you see how I've changed? Two years in prison will either make a man or break him. I have Melville to thank for my having survived it. He stood by me. He didn't arrange passage on an outbound ship so that I could escape punishment, for he knew better than I did at the time that a stateless, vagrant life is none at all. Melville is loyal—say what you like about him.

"Martin is a sensitive young man," said Ellen after a lengthy pause in the conversation, during which she'd been pursuing her own thoughts.

I wanted nothing to do with sensitive young men.

"Your friendship has done him good."

Feeling uncomfortable, I made no reply.

"Franklin and I have worried that he would get into some scrape he couldn't get out of. You can't imagine how vulnerable he is."

Oh, but I can!

"He has a good mind and heart, but I fear those qualities make him unsuitable for the Bowery. We would have moved to Staten Island if Franklin and Martin's father had not left them the house free and clear. . . ." Her voice trailed off, and what was unspeakable was left unspoken, or so I imagined.

I resented Martin for having drawn a pall over the sunlit afternoon, taking the luster from Ellen's hair and the brightness from her eyes. The lake water blackened, and the swans turned gray. The dream was nearly over, the opera at an end. Before the curtain rang down—possibly forever—I took Ellen's wrist and held it—too hard, by the pained look on her face. Having taken it, I could not let it go. If only you and I were going to San Francisco! If only life were otherwise! Ellen, you are my last hope. I wanted to say this and more, but I said nothing. In her wide-eyed look, I saw confusion, apprehension, and—I swear—curiosity. I let go of her hand. Without a word being said, we made up our minds to treat what had passed as a joke. She must have done so, because she laughed—not nervously, but lightly. And so I was saved from embarrassment and explanation. The Central Park was no more Arcadia than I was Silvius, or she Phoebe.

She stood and said it was time to be getting back. We found Franklin leaning against Oak Bridge, which spans Bank Rock Bay at the entrance to the Ramble. He was eating ice cream and, at our approach, smiled shamefacedly, like a boy caught committing mischief.

"Did you enjoy your walk?"

"We did until Shelby took advantage of me in front of the swans."

The color must have drained from my face, because Franklin took a step toward me as though he meant to crack my jaw. But then he broke into a laugh, and Ellen joined him, and I knew that they had been making sport of me and that I could have no significance to them other than as poor Martin's friend.

"I hope they didn't blush," he said, smiling.

"The swans are married, and nothing can shock them," she replied.

Now it was Franklin's face that reddened.

Ellen took her handkerchief and wiped ice cream from his mouth. "I declare my husband is a child! I dare not let him out of my sight!"

"My wife belongs to the National Woman Suffrage Association. Susan B. Anthony and Elizabeth Stanton are frequent guests at Maiden Lane."

Ellen humphed humorously.

"I've been typing early drafts of a novel for Henry James, *The Bostonians*. In it, a character named Olive appears to be in love with Verena Tarrant, a proponent of the woman's movement. Mr. James seems not to have made up his mind whether to admire suffragists and sympathize with women who find themselves in a 'Boston marriage' or frown on them."

"I expect any day to hear that Ellen has been arrested for conduct unbecoming a Christian gentlewoman and a professional typist."

"The Fiji islanders manage these things better," she countered.

Franklin picked up the hamper, and we left the park and caught a southbound train. A return ticket reminds us that life on earth is a to-and-fro business. But there is no coming back from eternity or the bottomless pit of time.

The Brooklyn Bridge's Manhattan Tower, May 9, 1882

I awoke at the Brooklyn Bridge, or so it seemed to me. I'd left Gansevoort Pier at the end of the day, only to find myself transported to the bottom of Fulton Street, in sight of the East River. By what conveyance I had arrived there—whether an omnibus, elevated train, or aeronaut's balloon—I could not have said. Like a man coming out of a mesmeric trance or an ether sleep, I looked about me in dismay at the iron doors leading to the stone vault inside the Manhattan anchorage, where wine merchants lay down expensive bottles of European vintage as if it were the niter-encrusted crypt in which Poe caused Fortunato to be walled up. The "Amontillado" that had lured me against my will—no, my will was in abeyance—was the impulse that had also caused Melville's Ishmael to "pause before coffin warehouses," and, from what I know of his life's story, had brought Melville himself to the brink of annihilation.

You must've contemplated it, as well. Sometime during your own entombment while you struggled with the intractable materials of granite, steel, and human flesh, you must have thought and thrilled to the idea of suicide. I prefer Hamlet's word: *self-slaughter.* I picture—forgive a ghoulish imagination alien to your own—a man, as might be you, me, or Melville, cutting his own throat and then the ardent blood pumping into a basin, or, say, eviscerating and roasting his own bowels. Nothing surpasses the medieval mind for ingenious tortures. Modern man, prosaic to the last, contents himself with a rope end or drop of arsenic. Roebling, it's butchery that I think of when I whisper that grisly compound noun from Hamlet's soliloquy, which— each in his own way—we all will utter.

I raised my eyes to the bridge, your monument to human ambition and resolve, and saw, in its granite towers, which soared into air once ruled by eagles, not cathedrals, but guillotines awaiting the heads of giants to lop off. Thus can the meaning of symbols change according to the mind's well-being or disease. I gazed at your bridge and imagined, in years to come, bodies dropping like stones into the river below. If the time comes when life cannot be endured a moment longer, I think that such a dying fall would be . . . I have no word to say what it would be. But it is better to jump from a sublime height than put a bullet through one's brain or nibble poison like cheese. I think that to jump from one element into another—there to have one's fire put out—is a more pleasing end than any offered by knife, rope, or rat bane. It was the death reserved for fallen angels, though the infernal lake was one of fire instead of the kindly water—kindly to accept us without demur, as a mother does the child at her breast.

My father took his own life. I rarely speak of it. When the panic and depression ruined him, the fire went out, and nothing I could say or do rekindled it. Like most men of business, he couldn't conceive of himself without one. I found him in his study, his Colt Walker in a lifeless hand, his finger caught in the trigger guard. He left no note behind him except for an ironic gibe on the frontispiece of his first edition of Barrett's *The Old Merchants of New York City*: "Gone to sell ice to the damned."

What would you be, Roebling, without your stones and cables, your tables and diagrams, formulae and the mathematics of your trade? Nothing. And it is in protest against this nothing that you've suffered martyrdom in this room to see the work completed. Melville, too, fears the nothing a man can become when his work is taken from him. He writes like a man possessed—desperately throwing his voice into the abyss and waiting to hear its echo.

I almost wish that I could walk onto the bridge and, stopping midway between Manhattan and Brooklyn, above the river belonging to them both, step off into eternity like a man poised on the gallows between heaven and earth, neither of which belong to him any longer. At the cost of a moment's terror, I'd be washed clean by the everlasting water instead of by strangers arrived to wash my corpse. I would die without the shame of a second infancy. If only I could give myself to the river, and, later, if my body be not found, to the ocean, where I would circumnavigate the globe, rolling in the deeps, at play with the calves, until my atoms merged with the water's and with theirs! What stays my hand? Is it the Dane's fear of violating "the canon 'gainst self-slaughter"? I doubt my reason is as pure as that. No, I'm afraid of the instant of pain, which, like the shattering of a stained-glass window, would admit me to an oft-imagined realm, where my damnation awaits. (According to the Calvinists, my end was determined long before my beginning.)

I'm not Hamlet or Ahab or even Melville. My passions are sized to the dimensions of a stock exchange, a trading pit, or a customs office on West Street, near the North River, where fraudulent men are exposed with the jubilation of Shylock sharpening his knife to take from bankrupt Antonio a pound of flesh. Once upon a time, I was a businessman in New York who hoped to become a merchant prince. The ambition having been a tawdry one, the failure cannot be considered tragic.

Do you really think I judge myself too harshly?

You're right, of course. A person is neither all one thing nor another. For an artist to claim he has caught his subject is a lie: The human essence eludes delineation and description. You might as well attempt to coax a cloud of smoke into a bottle as capture a person in words or paint. I suspect that my tale has not done Melville justice in the telling. To try to tell the story of a man is inevitably to fail and to make him smaller than life, which is, and must be, always larger than any one person's comprehension of it. Humans are not cattle to be shown and judged at a county fair. And yet, knowing this, we still pretend it is otherwise.

I foresee an unintended use for your bridge: a jumping-off point between this world and the next, at a place where two cities will either claim or deny jurisdiction, according to the fame or notoriety of the deceased. I agree that such an eventuality lies outside geometry, catenary curves, and structural analysis. I'd like to see an arithmetic that could account for it as well as other instances of passion and unreason. Such formulae, which rule over exceptions and singularities, nightmares and the dark motives of the heart, have yet to be devised. We can only shudder to think what might be done with them by the unscrupulous. Neither you nor your father is in any way to blame, Roebling, for the suicides that will surely come. Ideas once conceived cannot be unconceived. The Brooklyn Bridge exists not only in the space it occupies but also in the minds of men and women and—perhaps even more tenaciously and ineradicably—in their imaginations. Just so do Ahab and the White Whale exist beyond anyone's power to annul them.

Chapel of the Christ in Pike Street,
near the Brooklyn Bridge, May 9, 1882

Returning from the bridge and my contemplation of eternity, I paused at a chapel on Pike Street. I could see that it had once been a confectionary, but in place of sweetmeats, a shabby manger cradling a baby made of fired clay occupied the store window, together with a lamb missing a leg, which was nosing the holy infant with its woolly muzzle. By the yellowing handkerchief swaddling the child, the dust, and a bleached velvet drape behind the Nativity, I supposed that it had been put out at Christmas and then overlooked or forgotten. I pressed my nose to the glass and peered through the imperfectly drawn drapes, but I could see nothing of the room, though a light was burning within. I almost knocked at the window but hesitated, feeling afraid, as I had felt as a young boy made to sit in an empty church so that I would feel God's eyes on me and understand that no one can escape His notice or punishment, regardless of the darkness in which he hopes to hide. I was about to walk on, when the door opened and a man stepped outside onto the pavement.

"What do you want?"

I thought it was a question more fitting for a confectioner to ask than a minister of God, for so I saw him to be, although like the manger and the woolly lamb on the little stage behind the window, his appearance was shabby. His hair and beard wanted cutting, and his coat mending. He looked to be an old man, but I might have been deceived by his stoop and his drawn, pallid face.

"I'm not sure what I want!" I replied honestly. At that moment, I realized that I had been struggling with uncertainty, but as to its cause, I could not have said—not to him, not to myself. To say that I was "struggling" and to say "with uncertainty" was to understate both my struggle and my uncertainty, which had earlier in the day brought me to the edge of insensibility, beyond which lay madness or death.

Yes, I do sound like a character in a gothic novel. Underneath the gaudy language, one can find truth even there.

The man turned his back, and I understood that I was free to follow him inside the chapel or to continue on my way. It was not for him to encourage or discourage those who were washed up on his doorstep.

I followed him into a room where a dozen chairs faced a makeshift altar on which a cross bearing a gnarled-looking Christ, two tarnished candlesticks, a silver chalice, and a salver for the Host were arranged. Otherwise, the room was unadorned and as cheerless as the scale house on Gansevoort Pier. If God had ever inhabited this place, He'd fled from it long ago. Despite the man's neglect of himself and his show window, he was not unattractive. He possessed a magnetic quality, which drew me to him and, strange to say, to— Roebling, I must admit, however preposterous it sounds, that I sensed God in him. His coat—a U.S. Army chaplain's from the War of the Rebellion—had an unpleasant sour odor, and his hair and beard were rank with stale tobacco smoke, but in that squalid chapel, they could have served as frankincense. Had I been the impressionable sort, I might have dropped to my knees before him—so moved was I. Yet he seemed an ordinary man—less than that because the light in his eyes appeared to be going out. Maybe this is what finally determines our ordinariness: the deadness of our eyes. He was a man who had suffered—that much was obvious. I had the impression that he had suffered for his God—or possibly because of Him.

"It is weakness in a man not to know what he wants," said Winter. He also bore a name suitable to an allegory. He was leaning against the altar in a way that struck me as natural rather than irreligious. "It is, however, almost universal in our kind. Men who know their desires and obey them are to be feared. They are fanatical. To pretend to know God's and act upon them is the most dangerous and fanatical presumption of all."

"I know that I am not happy—"

"Happiness is beside the point," he retorted.

I asked him, indignantly, if he did not believe that a man or a woman was entitled to happiness. I might have been asking whether or not we were entitled to eat our neighbor because we happened to be starving. He was a strange man and a stranger minister, yet I felt compelled to remain in his stuffy room and listen to his sad commentary. If only he would have raised his hand and smote the altar or raised his voice and chastised me, I could have laughed and left him to his thunderation!

He seemed to forget I was there. He talked as if to himself. When the candles guttered and went out, he went on talking in the dark. He'd been a Lutheran chaplain in Grant's army and before that had served in the war with Mexico and in the Utah War, when "doughface" Buchanan sent an army against Brigham Young and his Mormon militia. Winter had seen much, and what he had seen had marked his countenance, his voice, and doubtless his soul. John Brown especially had affected him. Winter had been with him on the night before the abolitionist was hanged for treason and murders committed at Harper's Ferry. He had not been able to forget Brown or his injunction: "Even if you can no longer believe in the efficacy of Grace, in divine Providence, in salvation and last judgment, in the words of your calling, in goodness and mercy, you must *act as if you do believe in them*."

At last, he fell silent, and I roused myself and asked, "Have you no faith, then?" I was appalled to hear a minister of God speak as this man had spoken, even in that tiny room, with its tatty wares displayed in an unwashed window. I am not a religious man. In matters of faith as in economics, my attitude has always been laissez-faire. But his words had offended my sense of decorum. We were in the house of God, and it did not matter that the house was mean. Perhaps I felt His eyes on me again, sitting in the dark—the same dark as that of my childhood, because darkness is one and indivisible, whereas the light seldom arrives unaccompanied by shadows. "Have you no faith at all?" I repeated.

"Not as a child does," he replied calmly, "but as a man sometimes will for whom Christ has been worn to a splinter—or a matchstick, which he is saving for a night colder than he can bare, but whose ultimate efficacy he cannot verify without destroying it. My faith is a chill and doubtful possibility of salvation."

Winter had nearly let the fire go out in him.

"Not for an hour since that night have I forgotten John Brown or his words to me."

He talked about the aftermath of the late war, his disappointment in love, a daughter whom he had not seen in years, his itinerant ministry in the western territories, his loneliness, and his constant wrestling with God, who he wished would show Himself, even if he were to be struck down and damned by Him.

"I've often wondered if Old Brown was correct in what he said to me. To do wrong in the name of one's notion of right may be contrary to God's wishes. I believed in John Brown and the rightness of his cause. Robert E. Lee, who was in charge of the execution, believed in the rightness of his. Both were good and honorable men; both acted with conviction, though in pursuit of opposite ends. One of them, however, must have been wrong, since not even God can reconcile moral contradictions. I fear I may have been wrong to have praised a faith I myself lacked."

He was lost in his own bewilderment, and I realized that he could not help me. I was not even certain of my reason in having followed him inside the chapel. What *had* I wanted there? To confess? If so, to what? I ought to have sensed without needing to step inside God's hovel that whoever ministered to the souls of men in such a place would suffer his own torment.

Union Beach, New Jersey, on Raritan Bay, May 10, 1882

On Wednesday, Melville and I boarded the *Armenia* and steamed down the North River and onto Upper New York Bay. Castle Garden, where Jenny Lind had sung, and the Battery fell behind us as the ferry traveled through a stretch of water between Ellis Island and Governor's Island, menacing with the ramparts of Fort Gibson and Fort Columbus. Passing though the neck separating Brooklyn and Staten Island, I saw the highlands of the Navesink rise above the distant New Jersey coast. There in another age—thought savage by many, golden by others—Lenni-Lenape Indians had raked up oysters big as dinner plates and fished for blues or winter flounder, according to their season.

The steamer crossed into the sovereign state of New Jersey's territorial waters, named the Raritan, composed of the same atoms as New York Bay, as well as the Atlantic, whose salt mingles with them both. Annexation, possession, and division are the delight and raison d'être of governments, politicians, and cartographers. They are also qualities of men and women who seek, by addition or subtraction, to redraw the boundaries of themselves. To conquer and to be conquered by another's stronger will are two sides of the same penny.

Melville and I sat amid mail sacks and crates bound for Keyport, a town whose small harbor was the principal coastal port for shipments of New Jersey produce to Staten Island and Brooklyn, across the water in Lower New York Bay. Arriving at the slip, we disembarked as deckhands knotted hawsers around the iron bollards' rusty necks. The town was more populous that I had supposed. The dirt streets were lined with wood-framed stores and houses faded and peeling in the salt air. Wood lots of pine and spruce remind us moderns that Indians had once lived in the gloom of an ancient forest vanishing, sadly, into history's airless rooms. One day, only engravings and dioramas will be left to raise the past from the grave of time.

We boarded a 'bus, which traveled the bay's coastline between Perth Amboy and Sandy Hook, and got off at Union Beach, where the crippled steamer *George E. Starr* had run aground. She'd been harried by the *Wolcott*, a United States revenue cutter sent in pursuit from Jamaica Bay. After the *Starr* had foundered, the collector of customs had given

Melville charge of the valuation of her cargo, which included opium. I was accompanying him as the appraiser and bearer of the necessities of our universally despised trade.

The *Starr* had been making for New York City when she was seen by the lighthouse keeper at Sandy Hook, which marks the Atlantic's entrance into the bay. She had taken on contraband at Philadelphia and managed to slip out of port ahead of the revenue men. The *Wolcott* caught up with her off the coast of Brooklyn at Long Beach. She fired across the *Starr*'s bow and forced her onto the bay's Jersey side, intending to bottle her up inside Keyport Harbor.

Copper sheaved, the *Starr* was an old-fashioned clipper built in Baltimore during the Civil War. She'd been hauling freight across the Gulf until a smuggling ring purchased her. Like any topsail schooner, she was fast and agile and ought to have outrun the *Wolcott* except that her owners had chosen the crew for reasons having more to do with criminality than ship-handling experience. When they saw the revenue cutter bearing down on them, they panicked; the ship broached and heeled. The cutter drove her, as a dog does sheep, landward, where she grounded on a gravel shoal.

All on board her were thought to have swum ashore and fled into the dense pine woods. A platoon of marines from the Brooklyn Navy Yard had arrived and were searching them. A retired warship used to train recruits was lying off the beach to guard against looters. Given the enormous value of the cargo, the Treasury Department had no wish to see it carried off and sold piecemeal to Irish roughnecks at Hell Gate and in the Bowery.

"Opium-running is something new to these waters," said Melville as we stood on the beach and shaded our eyes against the glaring bay. "In 1816, John Jacob Astor smuggled ten tons of Turkish opium from Smyrna into Canton, enlarging the fortune he'd made in beaver skins. Since he wasn't evading taxes here, there was nothing to prevent him from getting richer there. What the government doesn't want to see is the Afghan trade setting up in New York City."

Two boys were standing at the water's edge, where exhausted waves—their energy spent by the distance they'd traveled from the ocean—dredged up pebbles and broken shells. Nothing is so interesting to boys as a shipwreck unless it be a house on fire or a dead horse in the street. I supposed that the pair of them was debating the question of how many pirates had drowned and concocting a plan to get aboard the *Starr* and ransack her for treasure.

A young woman, most likely their mother, had been raking clams and putting them in a basket lined with seaweed when she noticed the boys. She stood up, straightened her back, and shouted at them, "Max and Drew! Get away from there this instant!"

Naturally, the boys ignored her, and in a theatrical rage practiced by mothers of young children, she stormed after them. Holding each one by an ear, she dragged them back to the rake and basket while they screamed blue murder.

Melville laughed good-naturedly and said, "The only thing more vexing than a boy is two of them!"

Lizzie had borne him two sons. The elder, Malcolm, had

shot himself before he reached nineteen in the house on Twenty-sixth Street, where I had dined a month before.

Melville grew quiet. Perhaps the memory of his dead boy was going through his mind. Or maybe he was transfixed by the glancing light on the water or the shadows of clouds grazing on Staten Island's far hills. Or was he simply amazed at the way his luck had gone and his life turned out?

A waterman rowed us out to the *Starr* in his flat-bottomed boat. We stepped aboard and went down into the hold, where we discovered the illicit cargo and, crushed beneath a crate of machinery intended for a factory in the Mott Haven section of the Bronx, a crewman who had not escaped.

"Leave him be," said Melville. "It's not so warm today that he will start to stink. Let's do what we were sent to do, and then get the hell away from here. The marines will deal with him."

I agreed, and we set to work inspecting the cargo, a fair portion of which was the product of the poppy.

"Strange to think that something natural and pretty should be vicious," I said naïvely.

"The man who visited a brothel and came away with the Spanish pox probably said the same thing," he replied ruefully.

He unstoppered a flask he sometimes carried in his pocket, and we drank to "dissembling appearances." By the time we'd finished our work, we had also drunk to "*la vida breve*," "Walt Whitman and the 'procreant urge of the world,'" "Lucy Ann"—whether a woman or a ship, I never discovered—"Hawthorne," "the fleshpots of the ancient world," "Guttenberg," and the "fallibility of Galileo, who got it wrong."

"The world doesn't move around the sun," said Melville. "It revolves around each and every one of us. We are—every Jack and Jill—the center and fulcrum. And that, Shelby, is the trouble with the world and our damnable kind."

Both of us emerged from the stuffy hold with a headache and a brain fuddled by alcohol and fumes. Making a megaphone of his hands, Melville shouted to the waterman, who had been tonging for oysters while we were doing our best not for God or king, but for the United States Customs Service.

Melville gave a convincing imitation of a drunkard, and I felt that my own two legs could not be trusted. We sat forward of the dripping oyster baskets while the waterman expertly plied the sweep oar. Shortly, the boat scraped up onto the pebbly beach.

"I need a nap," said Melville, walking with the exaggerated fastidiousness of the besotted toward a stand of pine trees, where he flopped down, shut his eyes, and began to snore. It would have been a piece of low comedy had I not followed suit.

We awoke when the sun was setting fire to the western-facing windows of Manhattan, visible, if only to our mind's eye, whose vision is imperfect. We were parched and famished—words ordinarily applied to draught-stricken landscapes and cattle. Our heads had cleared of vapors, and we left the beach to find an eating house in Keyport. As we rode the omnibus back the way we'd come, I watched the wind darken Raritan Bay and ruffle it to chop.

We ate at Keebees, at the foot of the Keyport and Holmdel docks, which thrust into the Raritan like two splinters. I searched my mind for something to say that would interest Melville. At such times, I felt out of my depth—a goldfish in the ocean or a plumber arrived at Emerson's house to fix a leaky pipe during a meeting of the Transcendental Club.

"It strikes me as odd," I hazarded to say, "that a place should change its character according to the direction from which it is approached."

"What do you mean?" asked Melville, having pierced a fried oyster with his fork.

"I was thinking of Union Beach. It would appear to exist according to our view of it."

He lay the fork on his plate with a clatter, an invitation for me to continue.

"When we saw it through the open window of the omnibus, it appeared ordinary. But when the waterman rowed us ashore from the *Starr*, it seemed somehow exotic."

On such a beach, Robinson Crusoe began his twenty-eight-year ordeal on the "Island of Despair," at the mouth of the Oroonoque, visited, according to the timetable governing hunger, by cannibals. On such a beach, Captain Cook came ashore at Tahiti, and by Anna Maria Bay, at Nuku Hiva, Melville entered earth's erogenous zone, where shame was unknown to the tattooed inhabitants and the lurid colors of the birds and flowers could have brought genteel ladies to a swoon.

Viewed from land, Union Beach is no more than a cusp of sand lying against a bight of Raritan Bay. Seen from the water, it is anything you want it to be. The bridge rearing up outside the window, Roebling, is not the same one the sandhogs knew, laboring inside the caissons, or the people know who cross it. And the Herman Melville I saw across the oilcloth-covered table in Keyport was not the same man that others did. (And Gibbs? Always my thoughts return to him. I sometimes wonder if he existed apart from me, or I apart from him. Were we also Chang and Eng?)

"It is naïve to think in terms of absolutes in nature," replied Melville. "Emerson wrote of a 'radical correspondence between visible things and human thoughts,' whereby 'The dawn is my Assyria; the sunset and moonrise my Paphos, and unimaginable realms of faerie; broad noon shall be my England of the senses and understanding; the night shall be my Germany of mystic philosophy and dreams.' The universe exists only in relation to us, and our doom is to look at others and see only ourselves." His voice and still-handsome face were fretted by regret. "On second thought, there is one absolute in nature."

"And what might that be?" I asked.

"Evil. It is a quality inherent in nature, to which certain men and women resort. In that evil is not evenly distributed throughout living things, there must be a predisposition to it. Moby Dick was an absolute that compelled Ahab to dwell on it because he was predisposed to do so."

Abruptly, Melville changed the subject to the excise tax, as though his mind had been caught by a contrary wind.

"The tax on goods should be less than the cost of smuggling them," he said, "or it will behoove a person of greed and recklessness to attempt to circumvent customs."

"In an ideal world, there would be no need for an excise tax—or customs inspectors," I said.

"Emerson can write about idealism till hell freezes over, but it won't change the fact that our world is a fallen one. Accordingly, there are those who, unable to control their appetites, necessitate their regulation for the common good. In other words, Shelby, if bad men mean to run opium in ships, there must be a sixty-gunner to blow them to hell out of the water."

"Emerson died last month."

"I didn't know. Let's hope God is not a Calvinist after all."

At another table, two men were arguing the dualities of their bayside village life, a tiny Manichaean universe of clams or oysters, flatboats or dories, turnips or parsnips, Baptists or Methodists, lager or stout, draft horses or mules, fat women or thin ones from which to choose—good and evil seemingly having no part in their debate. To stay here, I said to myself, would be to cut the Gordian knot and retire to a life of simplicity. I said as much to Melville.

"Everywhere there are people, it's the same," he replied. "Whether you go to Timbuktu, Tierra del Fuego, or San Francisco, you'll find little difference among men, except, perhaps, for the color of their skin, their barbering, or tailoring. There is no running away from mankind, Shelby. More's the pity!"

In San Francisco, I was bound by probability to find another vicious brute to harry me. But I'd leave my shame behind in New York City.

We left the two men to debate their contrary faiths and heresies and the village to nurse its spites and grudges. Shortly, we were on board a ferryboat headed for Manhattan as evening began its shy approach.

What became of the sojourner among cannibals who wore skirts of bright tapa cloth, put bones and feathers in their ears, and scented their brown bodies with aromatic oils? Where was the sailor who had jumped ship in the Marquesas to escape a tyrannical captain, had been locked up for mutiny in the British stockade at the end of white-graveled Broom Road, on the island of Tahiti, had set bowling pins in Honolulu, hunted wild boar and picked breadfruit in the Typee Valley, and caught the spicy scent of citron and cloves from the gardens of Río? Does he exist—this man who once sailed into Valparaíso's horseshoe bay surrounded by twenty hills, walked through the white city of Lima rotted at the core and saw wild dogs scavenging corpses in an open pit? Does he still live within the aging man—the young one who sailed above the ruins of the former imperial city of Callao, drowned by earthquake and tidal wave a century before?

Melville was standing beside me in the bow of the ferry as the bay off Manhattan Island turned to gold, as it had for him long ago in Polynesia and in the Sandwich Islands.

Roebling's Second-Story Room on Brooklyn Heights, May 17, 1884

They're coming, Roebling!

The elephants—all twenty-one of them, with old Jumbo, the African pachyderm, in the rear, and Barnum, the world's most shameless showman, out in front, waving an enormous hat. They're parading along Fulton, making for your bridge. I see he's also brought along camels and dromedaries! The streets are mobbed. You must hate the fuss.

I never imagined it was *your* idea! But would you really prefer anonymity to fame, like Grant? I can't imagine Mark Twain wishing his name could be erased from his books. Melville would be gratified if he could be one of the famous dead and, like Tom Sawyer, able to enjoy the post-humous flapdoodle. Being forgotten grieves and embitters him. The rest of us welcome the forgetfulness of others. It is their gift to us.

Will you build another bridge or retire to Trenton? You've earned a sabbatical.

Of course, there's always work to be done and rivers to span! My friend, you look tired. Would you rather I left the rest of my story for another day?

"Get it over with," said the patient to the dentist, gritting his teeth.

The last time I was here, I noticed your rock collection. Did it remind you of the world's perdurable foundation, or its debris? Life breaks us all into pieces. If only we could be made whole with a dose of castor oil, a moral essay by

Emerson, or a sip of wine at the Communion rail! The Almighty could have laid out a less fatiguing road for His creatures to follow than that of obedience. He tested Eve's with an apple. "Shall I love God and forswear the fruit, or eat it and go my merry way?" She ate it, of course. Must we choose—always and only—between wicked indulgence and bitter renunciation? Must goodness taste like stale bread and sour wine?

I admit that, in former days, I chose indulgence, though I do not consider its having been wicked. I had a taste for parvenu society; as the son of an upstart, the upper berths of the Gilded Age were closed to me. I envied the perquisites of affluence and the confidence that only wealth can bestow. But I would stoop only so low to enjoy them. My father had been a war profiteer—a pygmy beside avaricious giants, such as Philip Armour, who made his first million by selling pork short, or Thomas Durant, who bilked the federal government by laying tracks in oxbows from Omaha to the hundredth meridian and proved that, in railroad building, the shortest distance to a fortune is not a straight line. It takes guts to climb to the top, as well as a willingness to be less than fastidious in all matters, excepting one's haberdashery.

Before the catastrophe, I was summoned to an informal hearing at the New York Custom House. Melville accompanied me as a sort of defense attorney—not for an instant did he believe I was guilty of wrongdoing. It happened shortly after our return from Union Beach. I was accused of having falsified appraisals. Such fiddling was often and easily done. I went before a tribunal presided over by Caruthers, collector of customs. Flanking him were the naval officer and the chief surveyor, both of whom seemed no more concerned than schoolboys would be in deciding the fate of a possum cornered by a dog.

I suspected John Gibbs of being behind the summons. He could have cast doubt upon my integrity by making a jotting in the ledger; he knows my business as well as his own. Melville also thought it likely. There was nothing to be done, however, and neither Melville nor I would risk a countercharge without evidence. I submitted, therefore, to the tedious examination by the collector, who spoke for all three men.

The U.S. Custom House at 55 Wall Street, May 12, 1882

"Mr. Ross, a serious charge has been brought against you,"

"Brought by whom?"

"Melville, that is beside the point."

"The reliability of an accuser is hardly beside the point."

"This is an inquiry, not a trial."

"Nevertheless, I insist on knowing the name of Mr. Ross's accuser."

"The charge was made anonymously."

Melville sniffed in amusement while I examined a picture above my judges' heads, commemorating the capture, in 1810, of the brig *Chelmers of London* by the French privateer *Junon*. The painting was a gift of General Lafayette during his American visit. At that time, the general also paid his respects to Melville's Gansevoort relations in Albany. Thus are we caught—the illustrious, as well as the least of us—in history's coils.

Caruthers unfolded a sheet of paper and shook it like a dirty rag. "I've a letter stating that Mr. Ross has been under-valuing certain shipments in collusion with their receivers in order to reduce the tariff due on them. And for his generous attitude toward some of the merchants of our city, he has been handsomely remunerated."

"Nonsense!" said Melville. "Mr. Ross is beyond reproach."

"Do I take it that you will vouch for his honesty?"

"Ross can be a fool, but he is never otherwise than honest. Does a dishonest man become a bankrupt?"

I thought his argument ill-advised, as did Caruthers.

"Very often," he replied drily.

Melville swept Caruthers's barb aside as one would a pesky hornet.

"Ross performs his duties punctiliously. His valuations are subject to my review. If you doubt him, then you must doubt me, as well."

"We appreciate your loyalty to a subordinate, Mr. Melville."

I hated to be called a subordinate, fool that I am.

"Not every one of my subordinates deserves my loyalty."

"What are you insinuating?"

Caruthers leaned forward in his chair expectantly; the naval officer played with a piece of string; the chief surveyor yawned.

"Not everyone under my supervision is honest," replied Melville matter-of-factly.

"How so?"

"By the law of probability. In that ours is an imperfect world and our species given to all manner of temptation and folly, it is likely that for every honest man, there is a dishonest one."

"You are uncommonly pessimistic, Melville."

"It's a rare man who can pass through the land of bilk and money and not get his hands dirty."

Caruthers cleared his throat in irritation and said, "I can see that nothing will be gained by continuing this discussion." He cast a jaundiced eye on me. "Mr. Ross."

"Yes, sir?"

I considered standing, as one does in court to hear his sentence passed, but on second thought, I did not think it worth the effort.

"Consider yourself admonished!"

I considered myself so.

"I trust there will be nothing set down against him in the record," said Melville.

In the space of five minutes, I had come to love the man.

"As you have pointed out, there is insufficient evidence. But we will be paying strict attention to the valuations of Mr. Ross and others working on Gansevoort Pier."

"And the author of that tattle? What do you intend to do about him?"

"As I told you, the letter is anonymous."

The hearing concluded abruptly, without as much as the rap of a gavel.

We stood once more in the briny air blowing down Wall

Street from the river. Melville said contemptuously, "For a moment, I thought Caruthers was going to put on the black cap and sentence you to hang. The ass!"

We rode the elevated up Greenwich Street as far as Gansevoort.

"Looking down upon tarred roofs is neither uplifting nor picturesque," said Melville gloomily. "There's no more splendid view of the world than from the topsail yard."

Preoccupied by the morning's unpleasantness, I merely grunted.

He must have sensed my uneasiness. "Why does Gibbs have it in for you?"

"We've had our differences," I said, hoping to sound nonchalant. "I bloodied his face on two occasions." I said nothing about the knife.

"I never took you for a brawler, Shelby!"

In spite of myself, I took pleasure in the compliment. What man wouldn't have?

"Beginning tomorrow, I'll make sure you two don't work together. I thought you'd be gone by now."

"Soon," I said, not knowing why I hadn't yet left the city.

"Don't wait too long, Shelby, or the moment might pass you by."

If it hasn't already come and gone, I thought.

West Street Customs Office, May 12, 1882

Gibbs and I were down in the hold of the *Harleem*, which smelled aromatically of flaxseed oil, considered a delicacy by the Germans, who spoon it on potatoes. As on previous occasions, he behaved as if nothing were amiss between us. Naturally, I was suspicious, and as the afternoon wore on, I grew irritable, until I could no longer restrain myself.

"Why did you accuse me of defrauding the Customs Service?"

He gazed at me as though I'd denounced him for having taken a balloon ride to the moon.

"I don't know what you're talking about!" he replied in astonishment.

"I was hauled before the officers of the port this morning to answer for myself. Or didn't you know?"

By his look of amazement, you would have thought that I was an escaped lunatic.

"And what did you tell Martin Finch when you visited him last week?"

I expected him to deny the visit, but as unpredictable as always, he replied soberly, "I wanted to see how he was getting on."

I laughed in his face. He took no offense, but, on the contrary, smiled warmly.

"His brother told me you upset him," I said, ignoring the attempt to ingratiate himself.

"I don't know why he would've said that. I stayed only a short time, and as far as I'm concerned, our meeting was amiable. Perhaps Franklin misunderstood Martin's mood. Did he say what I'd done to upset him?"

I shook my head, suppressing the urge to strike him again.

"We've all been asking ourselves why you haven't left for California—you and your friend. Has something happened to change your mind?" Had he pronounced *friend* in such a way that I should take offense?

I let my eyes probe his, but he was all solicitude, and I realized I could no more get the better of him than wrestle an anaconda.

"We haven't had a chance to talk about our trip to 'Aladdin's,'" he said with a sly grin. "To relive it in all its choice details."

I shivered, as though I'd been galvanized in the place where nightmares graze, appeasing their appetites on the memory of our crimes.

"I have nothing further to say to you, Gibbs!"

"I'll never forget the sight of you lying on the Turkish rug, your clothing in the wildest disorder! I've been to the Slide once or twice since then, and your *friends*"—there it is, that sinister inflection!—"wish you would come again. You made a very favorable impression on them, my lad. I was as proud to have been your escort as I am to be your friend."

I clenched my fists but forbore to strike him, knowing that it would give him a perverse satisfaction and stoke the fire of his enmity. The rage he had first shown, inside the hold of the *Saxony*, had turned inward. It lay coiled and waiting to unwind in a flash and rend his enemies. Smiling genially and talking of friendship, Gibbs had never been so dangerous as he was at that moment. Not content to insinuate, he became bolder as he worked the knife of his rancor into my vitals.

"I hope you will not blush, Shelby, if I allude to the special affection that one man will sometimes feel for another.

The prudish call it 'a sin' and 'an abomination,' but we know the truth of human nature better than those hypocrites. You and I understand the love whose name cannot be spoken and, because it must remain a secret, is undying."

Beware of the man who pledges his undying love; he can turn on you in an instant, if it profits him to do so.

"Well, Shelby?" His voice was silken. "Nothing to say?"

I turned from him and walked between the oaken casks waiting to be taxed. I would not let him see my hands shake.

The Finches' House, May 14, 1882

At one o'clock, I left the pier and went to Maiden Lane. I found Martin in a terrible state of nerves.

"Why haven't you been to see me?" shouted this timid man, who rarely raised his voice. "My foot is healed! We should have left already!"

"You seem in a god-awful hurry, Martin!"

"Have you changed your mind?" he demanded.

"No, I haven't." I paused, and then asked, "What happened the night John Gibbs came to visit you?"

Now it was Martin's turn to be evasive. He blushed and stammered and finally managed to get the words out: "He wonders why we haven't left for San Francisco."

"Is that all?"

He turned ashen and began to bite a fingernail.

"What else did he say?" I spoke sternly, like a teacher interrogating a schoolboy.

He made no reply.

I pressed him. "What else, Martin?"

He wouldn't answer. I let it go. I knew, without needing to be told, what had passed between them.

Why had Gibbs decided to go after Martin when it was me he wanted? Sitting in my cell, I had time to speculate on the whole sorry business and concluded that Gibbs's motives might not have been clear even to himself. He wanted to destroy me—that much was clear. By ruining my reputation, he could hound me into the poorhouse or an early grave. Apparently, his revenge insisted on Martin's destruction, as well. But was Gibbs driven by something else? I would not—could not—attempt an answer.

I managed to calm Martin with assurances that, within a week—two at most—we'd be boarding a transcontinental train at Grand Central Depot. I helped him into bed—he was as shaken as a child—and said good night.

Franklin and Ellen were waiting downstairs.

"Is he all right?" Franklin asked gruffly, in the manner of all large men whose feelings have been touched.

"Come into the kitchen, so he won't hear us," said Ellen.

She had made coffee, and when Franklin and I were seated, she poured three cups and joined us at the table.

"What's the matter with him?" she asked. "Who was that man who came to see him?"

"His name is John Gibbs; he works on the pier." I swallowed some coffee because my mouth was dry and because I wanted to postpone the lie I knew I would shortly tell. "Martin's his helper. Gibbs wanted to know when he'd be coming back to work."

"Doesn't he know that you two are going west?" asked Franklin.

"No, he doesn't."

You know how it is. We tell lies the way we burn logs to keep the wolves at bay.

"I don't approve of not giving proper notice," said Franklin, frowning.

"Melville knows, and so do the collector, the naval officer, and the chief surveyor. I met with them yesterday to give my notice, as well as Martin's, since he couldn't be there himself."

"Well, that's all right, then," said Franklin.

"I thought it better to keep Gibbs in the dark."

"Why?" asked Ellen.

"He's a mean-tempered so-and-so, who could make things difficult for Martin."

"I don't understand," she said.

"I've met his sort before," said Franklin, nodding over his cup. "It does no good to rub his kind the wrong way."

"Maybe he begrudges Martin his luck in getting away from the port. I know Gibbs hates his work."

"He could do something to Martin out of spite. You did right to keep it from this Gibbs fellow, Shelby."

I had satisfied the brother, but the sister-in-law looked doubtful. Women have an instinct for the truth, whether or not they choose to tell it.

"Are you sure that's all there is to it?"

"That's all there is." I hated lying to her, but what else could I have done?

We were silent awhile, each occupied with his own thoughts.

"When do you and Martin plan on leaving?" asked Franklin, setting down his cup.

I had been running my hand over the yellow oilcloth that covered the kitchen table. The sensation was luxurious, and I'd become insensible to the drama playing out around me.

"Shelby!" said Ellen, with a sharpness in her voice I had not heard before.

"Yes?" I must have looked an absolute fool.

"Are *you* all right?"

"I'm tired," I said, glad to speak the truth for once. "It's been a long day."

"Well, we won't keep you," she said—almost coldly, I thought, unless my imagination had gotten the better of me.

"Finish your coffee, then off you go!" said Franklin with his usual lack of insight into the secret motions of the heart. His question regarding Martin and my departure had been forgotten.

Are you beginning to disapprove of me, Roebling? Are you sick of this "confession," which seems to have no end? Every story is one made by its author—clothe it in raiment or rags, as he will. If it's any consolation, you'll never know if what I've been telling you is completely true or only partly so. One has to make allowances for the plot, which has its own power and obligations. To believe that life is plotless is to deny that the stars and planets have their fixed courses as they wander through the universe.

Roebling's Second-Story Room on Brooklyn Heights, May 17, 1884

I am sorry I couldn't have been here for the opening of your bridge. Melville forwarded the invitation to my cell in Sing Sing without comment. I've saved it for the sake of history and for the auction houses of the future, when the relics of our age will have acquired value. You see, Roebling, I still dream of posterity, if no longer of prosperity.

> THE EAST RIVER BRIDGE
>
> Will be opened to the public
> Thursday, May 24, at two o'clock.
>
> Col. & Mrs. Washington A. Roebling
> Request the honor of your company
> After the opening ceremony until seven o'clock.
>   110 Columbia Heights
>   Brooklyn
>
> R.S.V.P.

According to the *World*, opening day was the most splendid celebration the city had witnessed since the inauguration of the Erie Canal in 1825 and, years later, the Confederacy's capitulation. I heard about the great day from Melville, who would sometimes visit me while I was serving my sentence. My crime was other than conspiracy to defraud the U.S. Treasury. That affair had been settled by Melville's defense. In actuality, it was overtaken by events.

According to the newspapers, both sides of the bridge were mobbed by the curious, in their tens of thousands, many of whom had spent the previous decade in ridiculing both it and you. Almost all our sacred institutions were closed for the day—banks, businesses, even the U.S. Custom House, which reluctantly suspended its hunt for frauds and swindles. The stock market remained open in honor of a higher purpose called "profit." The roofs of Printing House Square, as well as those atop the Morse Building, the Temple Court Building, the Mills Building, and that owned by the *Police Gazette* were packed. Every window, doorway, and sidewalk was thronged, and boys were perched in trees and hanging like monkeys from the public monuments—all to watch the regiments and their bands parade through downtown Brooklyn and Manhattan. The best vantage had been appropriated by a solitary photographer sitting on top of the Manhattan tower. He was welcome to it!

The ships of the North Atlantic Squadron steamed underneath the bridge, as did the enormous excursion boat *Grand Republic*. The harbor bristled with masts and billowing stacks. The noise of artillery fire from the warships, answered by batteries at the navy yard, Fort Hamilton, and Governor's Island, resounded in Manhattan's cast-iron and granite chasms.

President Arthur, Governor Cleveland, and Mr. Edson, the mayor, led the parade across the bridge's elevated promenade to Columbia Heights. At night, Chinese lanterns in the trees were lit, their feeble light swallowed by the illumination of seventy electric arc lamps. Only the spectacle of the fireworks could distract the crowd from its admiration of the spectacularly illuminated bridge.

Melville described the celebrations in great detail. Even now I can close my eyes and vividly picture "The People's Day." I'm sorry, Roebling, that you had to witness it through this window. *You* should have been at the head of the parade, walking beside Emily, not Chester A. Arthur, the mayor, Cleveland, and two hundred other dignitaries, who basked in the vivifying effect of public acclaim as if they had deserved it. All those high silk hats bobbing down Fifth Avenue and Broadway—I'd much rather see Barnum's menagerie! The Irish protested. They are a pugnacious race and love rioting with a bottle or a stick of dynamite. The twenty-fourth of May also happened to be Queen Victoria's birthday, and municipal authorities feared that the "Dynamite Patriots" would blow up the bridge in spite, regardless of how many of their own had died or sickened in building it. Revolutionaries ignore contradictions and are fond of ruins. Having lost my place at the top of the mountain, I wanted to clamber up again—not to blast it into rubble. My mountain had been no more than a termite mound beside the Alpine summits lorded over by "Diamond Jim" Fisk, Rockefeller, or Vanderbilt, but a termite mound is taller than an anthill. After a stretch in Sing Sing, my old room in Mrs. McFadden's boardinghouse seemed like a palace, and I'd be living there now if she hadn't let it to an Irish road mender.

My story is nearing its end. What follows may strike you as incredible. Maybe it is. We'll leave it to the future to decide. Let us hope that the people there will be curious about us. I am pessimistic; it is easy to imagine an age that will repudiate its past, or—what is worse—not acknowledge it. The people will look at the dead without comprehension or recognition. "Who is this man?" a son will ask about the dead man who used to be his father. A young woman will come downstairs to breakfast and wonder who the old woman is, slumped over the table, her withered cheek lying in the butter dish.

The Finches' House, May 18, 1882

In the early-morning hours after I had sat in the kitchen and lied to Franklin and Ellen, Martin went to Gansevoort Pier. Other than a watchman asleep in his shack, the dock was desolate. Once again, the earth was taking on form as the night gradually withdrew beyond the western horizon.

I don't know why Martin would have gone alone to the pier. Whether in the hope of finding Melville and asking for his help or in obedience to Gibbs's command, I can't guess. He might have arranged to meet his tormentor at the scale house, with a mind to being rid of him once and for all. While I find it difficult to picture him confronting the older man on his own, fear can goad as sharply as desire, and cowards have been known to throw off their terror in desperation.

Melville opened the scale house door at eight o'clock and found Martin hanging from the balance beam. Questioned by police, the watchman stated that he hadn't bothered to look inside, because he knew it to be empty of freight— the cotton bales recently arrived from New Orleans having been forwarded to the mill on the previous day. And so it was that the assistant weigher was himself weighed. If he was found wanting in the scale of justice, only God—the collector and appraiser of souls—knows. Once I believed in universal justice, by which men and women ultimately got what they deserved. In this Gilded Age, however, the mechanism of reward and retribution is as readily tampered with as a grocer's scale. Ours is a time of false weights, false measures, false promises, and false hopes. In an age such as this, God will not stay the hand of Abraham, whose face is turned expectantly to heaven as he holds the flaying knife to the throat of his son Isaac, half brother of Ishmael, of whom the angel said to Hagar, his mother, "And he will be a wild man; his hand will be against every man, and every man's hand against him." So it has been since the days of Cain that men's hands have been clenched into fists or about the throats of their fellows.

When I arrived later that morning, I was greeted by Melville, who stood up behind his desk—a formality unusual for him. The American aristocracy, said not to exist, except in the imaginations of reformers, anarchists, and muckraking journalists, both courts and covets the old regime, to which Herman's father, Allan, martyred himself and his family in vainly trying to join it. His son would have none of it, preferring admittance to the society of successful writers, which insisted on excluding and finally ignoring him.

"You're white as a sheet," said Melville, coming from behind his desk and taking me by the arm. "Sit down."

He had just finished giving me the news of Martin's

suicide. I was leaning against my desk, dazed and wanting to be sick. Inside the office, all was still, as if waiting for instructions, while outside a wind was rattling the window in its sill. He took the flask from his jacket pocket and gave me rum to drink, and then we waited as if for something to happen that would cut us down from the hook by which we two seemed suspended. In spite of myself, I watched Melville's eyes turn inward, where his thoughts were revolving in their own eccentric orbits.

Finally, he broke the silence with an unsettling observation: "The horrific aspect of the case is that Finch hanged himself by degrees—piling weight upon weight in the pan at one end of the beam while the noose slowly tightened around his neck at the other end. He would have been lifted gradually up onto his toes and then beyond their reach of the ground, at which point he'd have been asphyxiated. The weights are still in the pan—the topmost one is the straw that broke poor Martin's neck. Thus was Giles Corey crushed to death by the Salem magistrates for his refusal to admit to witchery, as stone was piled on top of stone."

There is a sliver, a fraction, the merest hairsbreadth between the quick and the dead, I thought. If one day I were to write a story, I'd set it there—at the fatal intersection, where a remnant of life meets an intimation of death. I can't imagine a more excruciating crisis. What happens in that instant would test every metaphysical notion our kind has entertained since the first philosopher. Such a tale, if carried to its conclusion, could shatter worlds, never mind a human breast.

In due course, Martin's body was conveyed by a freight wagon to Maiden Lane, where he was washed, dressed, combed, rouged, and put on view inside a coffin plain as a Quaker's barn. Melville and I went and swelled a little group of mourners fitted into the parlor. Franklin stood stiffly in a new suit and starched collar, his arm protectively encircling Ellen's small waist. She sniffled; her eyes and nose were red from weeping. God forgive me, but I felt repelled by her mask of sorrow. Lying in repose, which churchmen and morticians call "eternal," Martin didn't look in the least as though he were asleep—an observation often made at wakes and funerals, by way of consolation. A halibut on a bed of ice at the Fulton Fish Market could not have looked any the less dead. The thoughts that sometimes enter, unbidden and unwelcome, into one's head are hardly Christian, though all too human. Silently, I apologized to Martin for my heartlessness and to Ellen and Franklin for my irreverence. I shuddered to think of my young protégé about to begin his tenancy in a plot of earth at Brooklyn's Green-Wood Cemetery, a destination that his parents and mine had already reached and to which Ellen and Franklin would one day arrive, each in turn, on board a hearse pulled by a black horse plumed with jet feathers.

Melville stood beside me, contemplating the floor. Is it the old trouble with your eyes that makes you downcast? I asked him in my mind. When I could no longer put off what the occasion demanded, I went to Ellen and Franklin and, taking their hands, mumbled condolences. Franklin appeared not to know me. Ellen took her hand away. A fly might have brushed her cheek, I told myself, or an itch have started requiring her hand's attention. I hoped that she had not recalled the afternoon in the park when, desperate and besotted, I held her wrist much too long and hard. Melville and I each drank a glass of gin punch set out for the mourners and left the house to its sorrow. I felt certain that I would never see her again.

In this, as in so much else, I was wrong. Ellen visited me in prison one dreary afternoon. She had traveled north on the Hudson River Railroad as far as Sing Sing. She was chilled to the bone by the walk from the depot to the penitentiary in a lightly falling rain. I won't bore you with the details of her visit, except to recall the sentence with which she left me—one that did more than a governor's pardon could to lift my spirits: "I'm grateful to you, Shelby."

I was certain that Martin had not done away with himself, but had been hoisted aloft on the balance beam by Gibbs, who was more than capable of murder and a grisly, ironic gesture.

"It was John Gibbs," I said to Melville when we stopped at the end of Maiden Lane to allow a dray to pass. "He murdered Martin and dressed it as a suicide." I had spoken abruptly, like a man for whom speaking the truth had been the furthest thing from his mind.

"What makes you think so?" asked Melville. He might have been asking why I thought the coming winter would be a hard one, he showed so little surprise.

I told him everything there was to tell: my fight with Gibbs in the *Saxony*'s hold, the knife, his having followed

Martin and me to the Battery, his drunken insinuations, the second blow I landed on his face, the bare-knuckle contest in the Bowery, my degradation at the Slide, his threat to expose me, his visit to Martin's house, the latter's terror and my misgivings. I didn't spare myself, and the odd thing was that Melville didn't appear the least shocked. I suppose that his youthful experiences had inured him to dismaying revelations.

"I doubt it can be proved," he said. "Gibbs is cunning, like all of his kind. There's no evidence or witness against him. The watchman claims to have seen nothing. No, I'm afraid there's nothing on which Auguste Dupin could chew." Melville did as much to his bottom lip and then said with finality, "For your sake, Shelby, let it go. The public will sooner forgive a murderer than a sodomite."

The vile word struck me like a blow, and I glared at Melville, who did not appear to notice my disgust.

"I'll see to the *Leander* this afternoon," he said brusquely. "You go home and compose yourself."

With those parting words, he started for Gansevoort Pier.

I had no intention of composing myself. I wanted to stoke my anger—to bring it to the boil and put it, hot and piping, at the service of revenge.

Yes, good people of the future, this is one of those old-fashioned stories—a revenger's tale worthy of Cyril Tourneur. Because I am stubbornly clinging to what is probably a foolish optimism, I'll suppose that you find such accounts of vicious passion incomprehensible in your enlightened age.

All that remains is for me to say how it was done, which

calls for another story. To tell it, I'll try to emulate the feverish tone that Melville struck in *Moby-Dick*. I refer the people of the future (assuming the book survives and there are readers to read it) to the last three chapters, which Melville—in the voice of Ishmael—devoted to "The Chase."

May 18, 1882, Gansevoort Pier (related in a heroic style)

Unseen, I followed Melville to the river, and while he was inspecting coffee bags down in the *Leander*'s hold, I was taking up the harpoon, which was leaning in the corner of our office. I threw it over my shoulder, as Queequeg would have done, and *strode* into the street. (This, the heroic chapter of my autobiography, requires a lofty diction.) On the pier, I went in search of Gibbs. To be absent so soon after Martin's death, I reasoned, would cast suspicion on him.

"Gibbs is cunning," Melville had said. Had there been a grain of admiration in those words?

"Why are you lugging that harpoon, friend?" asked the appraiser Toliver as I boarded the *Evangelist*, a Quaker ship carrying pineapples from the Caribbean.

"To kill rats."

He laughed and said, "There's big'uns down below, sitting quiet and waiting for the Holy Spirit to fidget them."

"What do you mean by carrying that pigsticker?" asked a merchant sailor leaning over the quarter-deck rail of the *Pelikan*, in whose hold lay sixty thousand pounds of Friesland pork.

"I mean to kill an evil whale."

The man scratched his head and looked at me as if I were mad.

I walked among the ships as Satan had among Job's herds in the land of Uz and the Lord had asked His fallen angel, "Whence comest thou?" And Satan had replied to Him, "From going to and fro in the earth, and from walking up and down in it."

I may have been touched by the madness of Ahab when I shouted at a sailor chipping rust from a Glasgow collier:

"'Hast seen the White Whale?'" It was the same question the *Pequod*'s crazed captain put to the master of the *Delight* in Melville's book.

The sailor stared but gave no answer. And yet I'd heard a voice reply, "'Aye, and I never saw its like before.'"

"'Hast killed him?'"

In prison, I would learn whole pages by heart of what I think of now as a demonic book.

"'The harpoon is not yet forged that will ever do that!'"

"'Not forged! ... Look ye, Nantucketer; here in this hand I hold his death! Tempered in blood, and tempered by lightning are these barbs; and I swear to temper them triply in that hot place behind the fin, where the white whale most feels his accursed life!'"

Accursed life!

I tell you, my as yet unconceived audience, that in my mind, I had grown gigantic, until I was proportioned like the bronze statue of George Washington standing on his plinth in front of the U.S. Custom House.

Then I saw Gibbs with his back to me at the end of the

pier, where it overhangs the river. I rushed toward him, careless of the noise. He spun around. A string of tobacco juice hung from his lower lip, which he'd been about to spit into the river.

"You!" he said. His tone was derisive, his lips, which he wiped on his sleeve, were curled in a sneer. "Have you come to pick my teeth with that?"

"You killed my friend!"

"Your lover, you mean."

"You hanged Martin Finch."

"The Elizabethans believed that the mandrake, called 'Little Gallows Man,' grew from a hanged man's seed spilled on the ground in a final rapture. I might go and pick some later; it's said to be a potent aphrodisiac. Your friends at the Palace of Aladdin would pay dearly for it."

"Villain! Why did you kill him?" My voice betrayed incredulity, when I'd intended it to be stern.

"I knew how much he meant to you."

He drew a knife. I threw the harpoon. It caught him between the ribs.

"'I stab at thee; for hate's sake I spit my last breath at thee. Sink all coffins and all hearses to one common pool!'" Ahab's words, or Melville's, but for the moment, they were mine by lordly appropriation and necessity. I had become Ahab smiting the whale. (Or was I the whale avenging itself on an insane antagonist who had harried it night and day? Symbols have a potency felt by readers in their blood and bones; they are more faithful to the mind's complexity than mere unvarnished truth.)

A jet of blood fountained from Gibbs's mouth, turning it to a scarlet grimace. Clutching the shaft, he fell backward into the North River. Briefly, he floated, the harpoon rising from his chest like a mast. His eyes saw nothing more of earth. What they saw of the world to come, I couldn't guess, save that his expression was one of horror. He gazed on hell or on the abyss, into which Ahab and the White Whale had plunged. Gibbs rolled over, and the weight of the harpoon dragged him down beneath the water's roiling surface until I could see him no longer. In my exultation, I sang an old harpooner's song:

> So be cheery, my lads, let your hearts never fail,
> While the bold harpooner is striking the whale!

So is evil served, I told myself, and knew that I was lying, because good can never get the upper hand in the contest between righteousness and wickedness.

I escaped capture on board a ship bound for the Caribbees, where I lived in contentment on a golden beach, eating fish and coconuts, admiring faultless sunsets, and siring a dozen brown children. Let's hope, Roebling, if you are awake, that the future to which my words are winging will be tolerant of differences and that our descendants will have finally found an all-embracing word for love. And let us hope—although I fear it is too fond a one—that none will abuse or be abused in the new Arcadia and murder will have become as antiquated as the flintlock musket. Well, Roebling, what did you think of my story?

Fallen fast asleep. You're worn-out by a madness of your own. It was more madness than malady, the thing that crushed you and from which you're not likely to recover. We pay a heavy tax to strike out on our own. Whether by ship, mathematical calculations, transcontinental railroad, or the Hudson River Railroad as far as San Francisco or Sing Sing—it scarcely matters. Must the people of the future also pay ambition's price, or will they be the beneficiaries of humankind's ancient struggle? Melville, you, Grant, even Sam Clemens ought never to have been allowed to fall into the pit of ruin—an arrears in Melville's case worse than what is set down in ledgers.

I hardly matter. I aspired no higher than to imitate wealthy gentlemen who play cards in private clubrooms, dress according to the latest fashion plates, intone doxologies as though they were on familiar terms with God, sitting comfortably in reserved pews inside churches named Trinity or Grace, and marry a handsome woman of their class—or if not inclined to matrimony, to live as gentlemen bachelors, admired for their gentility, sought after for their opinions, and courted by stockbrokers, rich merchants, and young upstarts alike.

And Martin Finch? He might have mattered had he lived. Or maybe not. Probably not. The mass of men and women don't matter except in and of themselves. Franklin was stoical in his grief; Ellen wept in hers what men deride as womanish tears. Evidently, Martin mattered to them. Did he to me? Yes, for reasons I have yet to comprehend. Let us hope that people ages hence will weep unashamedly for their dead and for the death of childish hopes.

The heroic tale of the destruction of an evil man named Gibbs is finished—told, however unsatisfactorily, in the manner of Ahab's fatal combat with a whale, whose ancestors were Jonah's great fish and, long before that, the great whales created by the Lord on the fifth day. God made them all, but who, I wonder, made Ahab?

Herman Melville did, one of the pygmy gods who rule the little world of books.

May 19, 1882, Gansevoort Pier (related in a prosaic style)

Now I'll tell a more plausible conclusion to my tale.

Like a monomaniac, I hunted Gibbs on the pier and among the ships, in the scale house and sheds. I searched Gansevoort Street high and low. I went to his rooming house on Charlton Street, questioned his landlady, collared and buttonholed pedestrians passing on the pavement outside the ramshackle house. That evening, I went to see General Grant.

"What brings you here, Mr. Ross?"

I could see that he was failing. That such a small thing— mere atoms of malignancy—should fell a man who had passed unscathed through the Civil War and endured two clamorous terms of the presidency! Say what you will of Grant, his life has been large and deserves to be extinguished by a leviathan.

"General, what is the worse sin you can imagine?"

"One that does not even have a commandment condemning it: betrayal."

Yes, I said to myself.

"Have you betrayed someone, Shelby, or been betrayed?"

"Both, sir." I'd betrayed Martin by not standing by him until after he'd been tidied and boxed up in his coffin. John Gibbs had betrayed me and my feelings for Martin, no matter how muddled and troubling they were and continue to be. (In addition, I betrayed that good soul Franklin and, in this effusion, I am betraying Herman Melville, whose soul I have plundered in order to furnish my own tale.)

"God forgive you the one and console you for the other," said Grant. His voice seemed to have come from a room other than that in which I stood with my hat in my hands.

Later that night, I went looking for Gibbs at the boxing ring and the Slide, where disgust nearly overwhelmed me. No one knew of his whereabouts. None cared to know. Thus are even the vicious betrayed by those who share their vice.

The next morning, I searched the pier and surrounding streets again. At noon, my mouth dry, I stopped at a taproom on Horatio Street, close by the river. There he was—Gibbs, drinking shots of whiskey with another man, a merchant sailor by the look of him, both men bound for stupefaction. Gibbs raised his face and saw me looming in the doorway (*standing* there—this is the prosaic version of my story). He looked surprised. Without a word—he was not worth the expense of breath—I shot him with an army revolver Melville kept in his office drawer.

The gun dropped from my hand. A woman screamed.

The merchant sailor scratched his bristly chin. I heard heavy beer mugs clatter against one another in the barmaid's beefy hands. Chairs scraped back on floorboards strewn with peanut shells. I heard a boy run out into the street and call for a policeman. I heard a gurgling sound inside Gibbs's chest. I walked over to his body—soon to become meat—crouched, and put my ear next to his mouth. I was curious to hear his last words; he said nothing, however. In death, his mouth hung open in a foolish grin, hung open like a gate on broken hinges. His eyes—a lovely hazel—stayed open, and if they saw anything, it was only the sooty ceiling.

June 2, 1882, Trial and Aftermath

Melville advised me to accept my sentence, which would, he felt sure, be a clement one because of the notorious personality of John Gibbs, which had emerged in testimony, however much it had been scrubbed clean of gross indecency. He was shown to be a bully who had persecuted Martin for his "inadequacy" until, having reached the limit of his endurance, he hanged himself. Even a steel cable will snap when the load exceeds its tensile strength, and Martin had little steel in him. On hearing of "the unfortunate Mr. Finch's suicide," my lawyer argued, I had lost my wits temporarily and taken revenge on "a thoroughly despicable person." Everyone involved in adjudicating my guilt or innocence was eager to settle the matter. The sultry atmosphere of a hot June day stifled enthusiasm for the entertaining spectacle of a man disgraced and fighting for his life. Had the torrid details of the case been made known, the trial would have dragged on until the reporters' ink ceased to flow and newspapers to profit by the lurid drama playing in White Street at the Tombs. Melville had counseled me—wisely, I now know—to say nothing of my suspicions concerning Martin's suicide, since the search for and discovery of evidence would have made a circus of the trial and ruined my reputation—and, more important, Martin's—beyond any hope of saving or repair.

So it was that, late in the afternoon, the judge rapped his gavel conclusively, and I was taken in a Black Maria first to the city's jailhouse and thence to Sing Sing to begin a three-year sentence for manslaughter, which was afterward reduced to two years because of my exemplary behavior and Melville's persistent advocacy.

Roebling's Second-Story Room on Brooklyn Heights, May 17, 1884

By now, the elephants will have all gone home to their chains and narrow stalls. Barnum is feasting with friends. I picture him at a table surrounded by Tom Thumb, resurrected for the occasion, a bearded lady, the Feejee Mermaid, Chang and Eng, and Jenny Lind. They are eating oysters on silver plates. They are drinking champagne. The sound of corks pulled from bottles is like that made by cannons fired across the water to raise drowned men from their graves. I hear Barnum and the others laughing while the elephants trumpet in sorrow.

I wonder what Barnum and his fabulous cohort dream. Is

it of the American Museum, reduced to ashes, from which it did not rise again? And the elephants—are they dreaming in their hopelessness of a green savanna beneath the African sun? And Melville. Is he dreaming in his bed of a great white whale? And what ancient dream coils like smoke in the brain of a whale? Could it be of Ahab, reckless and implacable? Or does the white whale swim though Ahab's dream until the earth is finally rid of men?

We cling to our stories like a mountaineer the rope that separates him from the chasm, or a drowning sailor the lifeboat that is his last resort from the abyss, or a man on trial for his life, knowing that only lies told with fervor and conviction stand between him and the gallows.

Pray for me, you people of the future—pray that I, who was returned to dust a hundred or a thousand years before your time, am at peace with the world and with myself.

Could I remake me! or set free
This sexless bound in sex, then plunge
Deeper than Sappho, in a lunge
Piercing Pan's paramount mystery!
For, Nature, in no shallow surge
Against thee either sex may urge,
Why hast thou made us but in halves—
Co-relatives? This makes us slaves.
If these co-relatives never meet
Self-hood itself seems incomplete.
And such the dicing of blind fate
Few matching halves here meet and mate.
What Cosmic jest or Anarch blunder
The human integral clove asunder
And shied the fractions through life's gate?

—Herman Melville, from "After the Pleasure Party"

ACKNOWLEDGMENTS

"... it is possible to imagine almost anything about a man
as tormented and great-souled as Herman Melville."

—Laurie Robertson-Lorant, *Melville: A Biography*

While they are grounded in historical fact, whose truthful-
ness is always doubtful, the books in the American Novels
Series are in no way biographies, official or otherwise, of
the literary and artistic figures they present. They are evo-
cations of their periods and their subjects—made real, or
at least concrete, by particularities of the events and places
depicted. The characters, drawn from literary history, are
not necessarily *as they were in actuality, but as they seem to
be to the narrator*, who is an unreliable one. The writing
of fiction has also given me license to elide and consoli-
date occasionally in the interest of the narrative. (In 1883,
for instance, Melville's office was located at Seventy-sixth
Street and the East River. I have stationed him at the 207
West Street and Hudson River office, where he spent the
majority of his years in the Custom Service, to simplify the
comings and goings of the characters. Henry James, Ellen
Finch's client, was in Boston and not New York City at
the time.) What I hope to accomplish with these novels

is to discover in our history the causes and beginnings of certain maleficent qualities in the American character. Since the writing is intended to be critical of contemporary life—at least of its vicious side, which is everywhere today apparent—it portrays the darkness at the heart of the nation's past. That past is an amalgam of American history, its literary history, of primary and secondary sources, and of my imagination.

I acknowledge the presumptuousness of believing I am capable of creating narrators and characters whose experiences are alien to my own, of drawing the vast American landscape, and of imagining myself within the minds of illustrious men and women, like a worm eating its way through the great books of the past. I gently remind readers that it is a presumption to write on any subject. But if the truth be told, I don't have an adequate defense for having written these books of mine. I am driven to do so, and it is for readers to decide whether or not it has been worth their while to read them and mine to have written them.

I gratefully acknowledge the authors and their works that I have chosen to represent nineteenth-century American literature—in the case of the present novel, Herman Melville and especially his *Redburn* and *Moby-Dick*—and other actual persons invoked, especially the silent auditor to whom Shelby Ross confides his story, Washington Roebling, chief engineer of the Brooklyn Bridge. His resolve, ambition, and suffering were as exceptional as Melville's own. I am also indebted to certain invaluable books read or consulted for the present work: *Herman Melville*, by Elizabeth Hardwick;

The Great Bridge, by David McCullough; *The Brown Decades: 1865–1895*, by Lewis Mumford; *Why Read Moby-Dick?*, by Nathaniel Philbrick; and *Melville: A Biography*, by Laurie Robertson-Lorant, a monumental piece of Melville scholarship to which I returned often. I thank Robert Fischler, historian, National U.S. Customs Museum Foundation; Gerald Weissmann, M.D., Research Professor of Medicine, NYU School of Medicine; and my friends at the Matawan-Aberdeen Public Library.

My obligation to acknowledge persons at the center of my life and thought is a pleasant one: my wife, Helen, well-wishers Eugene Lim, Dawn Raffel, Tobias Carroll, and John Madera, and especially Erika Goldman, publisher and editorial director, Jerome Lowenstein, founding publisher, and their colleagues at Bellevue Literary Press, Marjorie DeWitt, Elana Rosenthal, the diligent Molly Mikolowski, the patient Joe Gannon, and the scrupulous Carol Edwards.

ABOUT THE AUTHOR

Norman Lock is the award-winning author of novels, short fiction, and poetry, as well as stage, radio, and screenplays. His most recent books are the short story collection *Love Among the Particles*, a *Shelf Awareness* Best Book of the Year, and five previous books in The American Novels series: *The Boy in His Winter*, a reenvisioning of Mark Twain's classic *The Adventures of Huckleberry Finn*, which Scott Simon of NPR *Weekend Edition* said, "make[s] Huck and Jim so real you expect to get messages from them on your iPhone"; *American Meteor*, an homage to Walt Whitman and William Henry Jackson named a Firecracker Award finalist and *Publishers Weekly* Best Book of the Year; *The Port-Wine Stain*, featuring Edgar Allan Poe and Thomas Dent Mütter, which was also a Firecracker Award finalist; *A Fugitive in Walden Woods*, a tale that introduced readers to Henry David Thoreau and other famous transcendentalists and abolitionists in a book Barnes & Noble selected as a "Must-Read Indie Novel"; and *The Wreckage of Eden*, a story evoking the life and artistry of Emily Dickinson.

Lock has won The Dactyl Foundation Literary Fiction Award, *The Paris Review* Aga Khan Prize for Fiction, and writing fellowships from the New Jersey State Council on the Arts, the Pennsylvania Council on the Arts, and the National Endowment for the Arts. He lives in Aberdeen, New Jersey, where he is at work on the next books of The American Novels series.

BELLEVUE LITERARY PRESS is devoted to publishing
literary fiction and nonfiction at the intersection of
the arts and sciences because we believe that science and the
humanities are natural companions for understanding the
human experience. With each book we publish, our goal is to
foster a rich, interdisciplinary dialogue that will forge new tools
for thinking and engaging with the world.

To support our press and its mission, and for our full catalogue
of published titles, please visit us at blpress.org.

BELLEVUE LITERARY PRESS

New York